The Woman Who

Books by Kelly Cherry

In *The Woman Who* Kelly Cherry proves, once again, that the woman who feels is also the woman who thinks and creates and breaks new ground. Read this book for Cherry's unmistakable blend of heart-breaking emotional honesty and daring literary experimentation, united by a supple and complex faith.

—Trudy Lewis

The Woman Who consists of seven brilliant stories. Each pulses on its own, alive with lithe, muscular language and tough in its insistence upon honesty from, and about, its characters; each story is particular, sensual, and focused on human need while conveying a courageous philosophical inquiry. And each is a pleasure to experience. Read as a collection, united by Kelly Cherry's powerful investigatory impulse—what does art mean in a life? What does love mean in art?—*The Woman Who*, written by a polymath, one of our most distinguished inventors of life-in-language, is a stunning achievement.

—Frederick Busch

THE WOMAN WHO

Stories

Kelly Cherry

Boson Books
Raleigh

Published by Boson Books
An imprint of C&M Online Media Inc.

ISBN (ebook) 978-0-917990-59-5
        (print)   978-0-917990-60-1

For information contact
C&M Online Media Inc.
3905 Meadow Field Lane
Raleigh, NC 27606
Tel: (919) 233-8164
email: cm@cmonline.com
http://www.bosonbooks.com

Designed by: Jocelyn Tiller
Cover image: *Green Cathedral* by Joel Barr

Contents

Acknowledgments

Six of the seven stories in this collection appeared in different form in my novel *The Lost Traveller's Dream*, in which they had been embedded, at editorial behest, without titles. I have extricated this material and returned the collection to its original status as a group of individual short stories. I have also taken the opportunity to revise freely. In several instances, the titles under which stories had previously appeared in journals or magazines have been changed. "Her, In His Story" appeared under a slightly different title in *Shenandoah* and is collected here for the first time.

As so often, the Virginia Center for the Creative Arts generously extended to me a residency, during which I worked on this project. I wish to express my heartfelt thanks to Nancy and David McAllister for making this book happen. My husband is my first, second, third, fourth—and so on ad infinitum—reader, and I owe him everything.

WHERE THE WINGED HORSES TAKE OFF INTO THE WILD BLUE YONDER FROM

I am in an observation car; what I am observing is North Dakota.

The first time North Dakota existed for me was ten years ago and thousands of miles away. I was staying at the Metropole in Moscow, and met an American fur trader who was there to do business. It was January and I was expressing admiration for the weather, at ten below. "My dear Kathryn," the fur trader said (he sported a Stetson on his silver head but his manners were entirely Continental), "this is nothing—a little nippy, that's all. You won't know what cold is till you come to North Dakota."

He presented me with a sample of his wares—fur-lined gloves, but they were two sizes too large. Later, on the train to Berlin, I gave them to a medical student from Madagascar; he was on holiday from Patrice Lumumba University. The news had just reached us that several European nuns had been slaughtered in a revolutionary action in the Congo, and the med student was trying to stir his traveling companions to a kind of applause on behalf of the Third World. I gave him the gloves because I had already learned that everyone can be bought, even Marxists.

That was a loud, crowded train; this one's quiet. Or maybe it's just that I can no longer pass for a college student, and so am excluded from groups. These days I tend to keep to myself when traveling, and certainly when traveling through North Dakota, although not long ago John Barth autographed my copy of *The Sot-Weed Factor* in Grand Forks. "To Kate." That was the second time this state became real for me. Thus does the mind's map achieve scope and detail, rock by rock, tree by tree, ridge by ridge, telephone pole by telephone pole. Aristotle quotes an earlier philosopher who said: "As more and more things come into being, the universe, taken as a whole, swells."

Now I am having my third view of the Prairie Garden, *en passant.* I am on my way to Seattle. The reason is simple—it's the same motive that's sent me everywhere I've gone since 1965. If I can't be in the one place on the planet I ought to be, I might as well be anywhere. Here is anywhere. In fact, for all I know, by now it could even be Montana. In the distance there are mountains shaped like pyramids rising from the flat earth.

* * *

The *one place* is with Pēteris, in Latvia, one of the three Baltic republics that came under Soviet domination as a result of the war. I would emigrate—ask me my political party and I'll say "realist"—but they won't let me. As for who "they" are, they are the same folks who censor our mail, on both sides. England is the only major power not censoring incoming mail; there, reading other people's correspondence is uncivilized, not to say uncouth. But between the U.S.S.R. and the U.S.A., the iron curtain is like a lead blind. Détente isn't just a word; it's the promise of light. But the way those things work— Look, change starts at the top and filters down like meltwater through topsoil, and by the time it reaches the rest of us, it's been refined out of existence.

Yet Pēteris wrote me that as time goes on he remembers me with increasing clarity, seeing in his mind my way of walking, talking, and saying his name. I worry whether time hasn't also refined his image of me, but for my part, I depend on his testimonials of love the way a hemophiliac depends on transfusions, utterly. When we met, I had already been bleeding for years, having been wounded at an early age. Pēteris knows this tawdry fact about me and isn't put off by it. Where less desperate couples make suicide pacts, we agreed to a life pact; for each other's sake, we would endure the flak, shit, and pure grief that piled up, like dirty snow, in both our lives.

Periodically, Pēteris enters a hospital—on account of his drinking, but also because he becomes convinced that his brain is being flattened out by boredom like dough by a gigantic rolling pin. He drinks to make himself stupid, since the stupider he becomes, the more fascinating everyone else in his world seems, and the more the world fascinates him, the more alive his intelligence becomes. It's a paradox, and perhaps that's why the psychiatrists at the hospital have so much trouble grasping it. On the other hand, where the psychiatrists fail, I succeed, and between the fifth and sixth paragraphs moved downstairs to the bar car.

With a slight buzz on, my own mind runs risks it might never otherwise brave or even recognize, and I drink and stare out the window and think about things like love and marriage and where the winged horses take off into the wild blue yonder from.

Hospitals are one of the things Pēteris and I have in common. I used to think I was dying. Once I went to St. Luke's and waited four hours in the emergency room for the chance to inform a doctor that I was having a heart attack. He peered into my pupils so intensely I was afraid I might kiss him, out of reflex. But he backed away, making me feel ugly and rejected. This was during one of my crazy periods. Nevertheless, most of the time I'm sane enough, if sanity consists in working hard, being friendly to your fellow man, and meeting obligations. Of course, sanity is patently insufficient. Several hundred thousand people will starve to death this year, and the only way I could help would be by giving them my body for food—and unless somebody performed a miracle on it, which hasn't happened in a long while, it wouldn't go very far.

***

The first time I saw Pēteris, I was waiting for the coffee shop in the Metropole to open. He told me he knew I was American by the manner in which I lit my cigarette, striking the match prudently outward from my body. I knew he was watching me. I think if he had simply approached me, sat down beside me on the couch, kissed me deeply and touched my back and neck, I would have made love to him on the spot, with an inappropriately languorous concentration.

The coffee shop opened. I maneuvered myself in line just ahead of him; he was dark, tall and thin, strikingly good-looking but obviously profoundly self-willed, with a Vandyke that spelled danger. But his intentions were unthreatening. Besides, he was with a friend. We started talking and wound up leaving the Metropole together; he hailed a taxi, which we took to a bar across town, engaging in hectic conversation made inexplicitly poignant by his friend's use of sign language: She knew no English and had once worked for a deaf-and-dumb retailer. The friend was very pretty, a tiny bit stocky and as sweet-tempered as Grushenka. At once, I was jealous of the friend's role in Pēteris's life and proud of Pēteris for eliciting such plainly tender concern. I wanted to express my own feelings, but was young—the same age he was, twenty-three—and needed to know how he felt about me before I would risk revealing how I felt about him. It was a matter of disarmament.

***

A number of men, including my ex-husband, have acquainted me with myself over the past ten years, but when I was young I assumed that lovers, calling me beautiful, lied like sons of bitches, for the fun of it. Whatever capacity for enchantment I had couldn't be pinpointed in a mirror; it showed itself in my idiosyncratic intelligence, in my jaw's jut (a family trait), and in a certain whimsical pelvic slant which was, however, not so much eager as innocently receptive. At first, I didn't know what I looked like; later, I realized I had been beautiful, and regretted time's erosion; lately, I've learned to look outside myself, enlarging my world. For example, I notice that we are climbing. Up and up—the sky's the limit. Look! The mountains are here, lit by incandescent clouds. The mountains glow; light breaks on their snowy peaks like waves on a beach and rolls down; cattle graze in the green valley. When the clouds part, the sky falls back. It falls back a million years, into sheer space, but down here the grass is speckled with sweet peas and buttercups, and clumps of dandelions mottle the hillside. We're in Glacier Park, crossing a ravine. It's a dead drop, shale and air all the way. In that cup of earth, light comes and goes; it runneth over; light brims and spills onto the tops of trees. The leaves sparkle—I record this and other impressions, thinking that someday I will tell them all to Pēteris.

***

We thought someday we would be together. Now here I am, moving ever farther off. Years and miles. It's not right, this separation. We were meant for each other, and I don't care who hears me say it. One more drink and I'll tell the bartender.

***

Pēteris has been married three times. He wrote me that he first fell in love at twenty; they had a fight, in which she said she didn't love him. To make her live with what she'd said, he married her sister. The sister didn't love him, nor did he love her, but they lived together for a year and produced a daughter.

His second wife was very beautiful, breath-taking. She bore him a second child. She had nothing more to recommend her, however.

(He was divorced from the second wife for about six months when we met in the lobby of the Metropole Hotel.)

He picked out his third wife at a party his friend Mirdza took him to; a lot of theater people were present. His wife-to-be was a dancer, the type of the corps, small, round, and strong, disciplined and doll-like. Actually, he didn't marry her until they'd had three children and needed to apply for a larger apartment, but from the beginning he was unwilling to love a woman without living with her. And he did love her. I knew that. He had turned to her when I wrote him I was marrying Ezra.

Pēteris had taken his diploma at the conservatory in Liepāja, and the first summer after my visit he stayed on there, in a cottage by the seaside. His salutation was always "Dearest Katiņa." The second summer, he traveled back and forth across Latvia with a theater group, intending to write music for plays. He had some new ideas along this line and wanted to try them out but—as he wrote later—something went wrong with his nerves and he had to abandon the idea of working. He found my letters when he returned home and wrote right away, but I had meanwhile concluded that he'd forgotten me—or at any rate, that he only enjoyed the romance of my being in America. Until recently, I always expected the worst. (Thinking things over, I've come to the conclusion that nothing's predictable and that we therefore must allow at least the possibility of right occurrences.) I thought he had become bored with the idea of me. Meanwhile, I observed that Ezra Solomon, a visiting instructor in art, was mad for me—and at me. He seemed to hold me responsible for the way he felt about me. I ran into him at a party and he acted as if I didn't exist, although I was sitting in a chair not two feet away. He and his date were on the floor. Janet, the date, said she was thinking of running away to Australia; surprising everyone, she did just that, a couple of months later, once sending me a postcard from Sydney with a kangaroo on it. But that particular night, she was insistently present, long dark hair ironed flat falling from a center part, the crown circled by an Indian headband. My hair was long then too, but no longer than to the middle of my back, and it wasn't black but brown,[1] and I wasn't hip, and probably was not even as scared as she was, though like all of us in those days, I wasn't above trading on my phobias.

Ezra still hadn't acknowledged me. His sexual style was intense-ugly, owing much to Jean-Paul Belmondo. He

---

1 I'm Scotch-Irish, English, Welsh, French, and Portuguese.

kept a hand on Janet's shoulder and chain-smoked with the other, and when I said good night, he gave me two fingers in a salute that was half comradely and half obscene.

***

When I wrote Pēteris about Ezra, I was hoping for a certain kind of reply, one that would convince me he had meant what he said. It came—the week of the wedding. Ezra and I were already at my parents' house. I didn't have the courage to call it off. And what could I say, anyway? That I wanted to marry a man I'd known for four days, who incidentally lived behind the iron curtain? Katie Allen, Bolshevik. In high school I was a lieutenant in the Civil Air Patrol. We had about twenty-five members and we used to march up and down the Midlothian gym on Thursday nights. The idea was to train young people to be on the watch for enemy fighter planes, in case of a surprise attack. Not only did I get to march—the big plus was that as a result of my militarism I got asked to the ring dance at John Marshall by a real cadet. He dropped the ring. Terrific. It rolled down the length of the figure and he had to chase after it. He put it on my finger but later, introducing me to his parents, he said I dropped it. I let him get away with that because I didn't want to embarrass him in front of his parents. Then for the rest of the evening he acted as if I didn't exist (that happened to me a lot), and before it was over I found him making out with a blue-eyed blonde in the back bleachers. I guess he had to show me he was a man, in spite of the ring. He was sixteen. I never learned to tell one airplane from another and in any case I thought I'd rather be red than dead.

***

Before I would accept Ezra's proposal, I said I had two questions. One was if he wanted kids; the other was if I could visit Pēteris the following summer as I'd planned. He said yes to both, but I was to learn he passed my little test dishonestly, never really willing to commit himself to children, and never really intending to let me go off to the Soviet Union to visit Pēteris. Even after living expenses ate up the money I had saved for the trip, Ezra kept poking around in my brain as if I'd tucked away the hope of Pēteris like a rainy-day savings account. It was ludicrous; hadn't I chosen him, and besides, wasn't the world inhabited by plenty of attractive men, all nearer? Talk about paranoid.

We moved to Brooklyn Heights. I took the greatest pleasure in this apartment. The walls were stark white (it's not true that walls have to be off-white), the trees sent their sweet smell up from the street,[2] everything, including life, was clean, and even the Michelob sprinkler bottle was beautifully shaped. One summer night while I was ironing, Ezra sat down at the piano, as discordantly as Dostoevski's Underground Man, as if to prove that *Homo sapiens* cannot be merely a piano key since he is the piano player. I asked him to stop; I felt like a harridan but for some months my sensitivity to sound had been increasing. That was one of the reasons he was sending me to a psychiatrist. My father is a musician, my mother is a musician, Pēteris is a composer—I didn't need a psychiatrist to tell me why

---

2 When Khrushchev came to New York in 1960, he—that mass murderer—remarked, "There is no greenery. It is enough to make a stone sad." But he didn't get down to Brooklyn Heights. We were on the fringe.

suddenly a pin dropped, a sigh, became an explosion and storm.

"What you really want," Ezra said, despairingly, "is for me not to exist."

"That's not true!"

"The hell it isn't."

I felt defeated, immobilized. Part of the problem was that he was always right, from one point of view, but there was always the other angle he refused to see things from. I had been accustomed to ambiguity; now I was told nothing meant everything. Instead, everything meant one thing—the center of the world was my "repressed hostility"; a splenic glare erased the shadow of option from my world, and I found myself moving in a two-dimensional field, where surfaces were cold, shiny, and deceptive. I was becoming unpleasant, finding life in such an unforgiving light too tense. I developed an ulcer, became accident-prone—

I burned my hand on the iron and ran into the kitchen to smear butter on it. Then I wrapped a dishtowel around it. It still hurt. I was crying.

"That's an old wives' tale," Ezra said. "You should hold it under cold water."

The thought made me wince. Like his practicing. "You don't know," I whispered, "what it sounds like in my head. I'm not making it up."

"I didn't think you were." His voice grew rich and sorrowful. I thought it was vastly more musical than his piano-playing.

He went into the kitchen and then I heard him say, "Shit," and then he said, louder, "I'm going out to get cigarettes," and I heard the door opening and shutting. I took the towel off and looked at my hand. It was red and greasy but it no longer hurt.

***

In Riga, Pēteris applied himself first to an oratorio and then to a new symphony, but things began to go wrong at home. Some of this he wrote me about, later. Some I sensed, or extrapolated from my own situation with Ezra. He increased his drinking, passing out at an awards ceremony in Budapest. It wasn't the kids—he was crazy about all the kids. So was his wife. The problem was between him and her. It was just, they bored each other; it was as if each day they were dying, side by side, in silence. She screamed at him, and since he could only assume that he deserved her wrath, he said nothing. Or he said the hell with it and went out, like Ezra. Sometimes he'd pick up somebody, but his wife never acknowledged this. After a while, they learned to respect each other for being able to take what they dished out to each other. He admired her independence. She was very well liked and he felt all their troubles were his fault. But there was no one he could tell this to or be absolved by, except the shrinks at the hospital, and they were so unimaginative they couldn't even comprehend the logic of addiction.

I tried to fit these facts about Pēteris into my general knowledge of the Soviet Union. Citizens eat ice cream on the sidewalks in winter. Divorce between consenting parties costs about $150. To see Rembrandt, go to the Hermitage. Alcoholism is a national epidemic. There are no stoppers for the drains of sinks and tubs in the Soviet Union. Black tights are the sign of a whore. The KGB fucks everyone; therefore, you must learn to love the KGB. In Siberia, houses have walls that are three feet thick, and the Fahrenheit temperature hits ninety below. Sometimes, the setting sun strikes the snow crystals in such a way that the trees and fields seem to catch on fire. There is a terrible ache in the citizens' hearts.

***

When Ezra left me, I wept for three days straight. I quit eating and went down to eighty-eight pounds. I looked in the mirror and asked myself what I thought I was doing. Did I think I could get him back by clarifying my position as victim? He might be a Jew, but he was a fascist son of a bitch. I tried to laugh at myself, but my throat closed up the same way it did when I tried to eat.

The most hilarious thing was when I sent a cable to Pēteris, asking if he still wanted me. He wrote, "I have a wife and baby, and I love them very much." Of course, he wasn't yet legally married. But what was a piece of paper, if it hadn't kept Ezra from leaving me?….

So I had done myself out of them both. I thought I deserved this irony, and called it poetic justice. I retreated to my parents' home in Richmond and they bought me a puppy.

***

The telephone rang at 4:00 A.M. I had been asleep for barely an hour and was reluctant to wake up. The operator said she had Moscow on the line.

"Come to Russia," Pēteris said, "or I kill myself."

"Look"—I meant to explain things calmly, be rational and precise—"you can't talk to me like this. You have a wife."

"Yes."

"Well, then, you shouldn't make phone calls like this."

"I love you."

"You're drunk."

"Yes," he said, amiably.

"I don't have the money to come to Russia. I have to go to work in the morning."

"Come to Russia or I die."

"Pēteris!"

"Katiņa," he said. "Say you love me."

"I can't, I don't have the right to." That was stupid of me, but more than righteousness was involved. I was afraid that if Pēteris saw me he wouldn't want me anymore. At the same time I distrusted young men's attitudes toward me, I had been one of those girls who could count on their looks, even economically. It used to be, when ticket sellers saw my face, they volunteered the best seats in a supposedly sold-out house. Landlords reduced their rent and repaired the kitchen fixtures, without laying a hand on me. Flower vendors pressed bouquets on me free of charge. In my sick moods, I thought they felt sorry for me. I even thought, Maybe Pēteris feels sorry for me or is making fun of me. I didn't truly think so, but I had to admit the chance. I had, after all, been wrong before. Take Ezra. It was best to warn Pēteris that I was losing my looks. "I'm skinny," I said. "I'm getting old. I'm one of thousands of frantic female singles in Fun City. I am disappointed in myself."

"Me too," he agreed, undeflected. "Is very sad. Dream and reality, they are unstickable things in a biological together."

"Absolutely," I said.

"Katiņa," he said.

"What?"

"Come to Russia, or I kill myself."

***

We'll arrive in Seattle shortly. I'm embarrassed to see my waiter from last night; today, I realize I was too looped to figure twenty percent and gave him a three-dollar tip on a six-fifty meal. No wonder he grinned. He said I was getting "the finest service north of the Mason-Dixon line." I remember the first person I met in Moscow, a student from Ghana. I had just got there and left my room, thinking I'd go for a walk. I was standing on the street when he approached. We took the bus to a cafeteria. Over a glass of tea, I asked him which he liked better, Ghana or Russia. "One always loves the Motherland," he replied.

Anyone could be eavesdropping; the student himself could be an agent; it was 1965, between regimes, and no one knew where things were headed. I decided not to ask which was the Motherland.

Boundaries baffle me; civilization baffles me. Cro-Magnon man could travel anywhere he liked, so long as he was careful not to be eaten up along the way.

The land itself is nonpartisan. It's also direct in its statement—white patches against black rock, green grass under a blue sky. Creation speaks its one word, the Logos, saying everything worth saying. The most any of us can hope to be is a translator. Some sentiment lodges in your heart like sand in a shell, and you spend the rest of your life seeking to render it into abstraction. *Es mīlu tevi*, Pēteris; *es mīlu tevi*, God; *es mīlu tevi*, all peoples of the planet.

***

The sky is overcast—it stays that way all the time I am in Seattle, or, rather, Port Townsend. I was met at the station and ferried over, an act that always gives me the shivers. Rain hangs in the air; it's the middle of June but it's as cold as December in New York. I haven't had a letter from Pēteris in days. When that happens, I worry whether I ever will. I never doubt his love anymore, I'm not so arrogant anymore, but I think about the KGB, the CIA, LSD; I am hounded by initials; the papers are full of our country's complicity in assassination plots, how the army tests drugs without right or consent.[3] I worry about his health. Last year, I learned he was in the hospital and for the first time confronted the idea of a world in which he didn't exist. It was horrible, a blank world, an unwritten world. As it turned out, he was in the hospital only to dry out; he hasn't had a drink in months. But the lesson remained with me, that the sentence you don't say is the one nobody hears. So I wrote him that I hadn't forgotten him, and that was all he was waiting for. He talked it over with his wife and moved out. I don't know what happens now—I want to live there. Friends say I'm crazy, that I'm renouncing my career. I say, Good riddance. Besides, it's only the work that counts.

***

On my way west, I stopped in Warsaw. The hotel was huge—and deserted. I wandered up and down the corridors, looking for a bathroom. When I finally found one, it had the biological symbol for "woman" on the door; across the hall, an opposing door was marked with the symbol for "man." My head ached; my throat was sore. I was coming down with a cold, and went into the dining

---

3 Army Intelligence cross-examined acquaintances of mine when I was in the Soviet Union, intimidating my landlord so that when I returned he asked me to move immediately.

room in search of aid. After fifteen minutes of explanations, I managed to convey the concept "juice," and after fifteen more long minutes, a delegation of waiters returned from the kitchen with a wine decanter filled with orange juice. I forked over a small fortune in zlotys, took up my decanter, and retreated to my room, where I spent the weekend in bed, wondering whether I should call up the American Embassy and make them send me home.

Home is a word I use from habit; I have no home. There is only the one place I ought to be, where I am not. Things could be worse. He could be Albanian.

Still, as Ezra suspected, there's always hope, and I order my life always to leave room for Pēteris in the future. This occasionally means restructuring the past, as when I legally forwent the name Solomon. I called Ezra to let him know (I also wanted to make sure our Mexican divorce was correct and unarguable). The hatred in his voice! I may be a pain; I don't think I earned that extreme animosity. You'd think he would have calmed down by now. I have; Ezra seems accidental, a quirky, unpremeditated complication, not tied to my soul by the same definitive meanings that make Pēteris as necessary as air, as essential as light.

I don't know where those meanings come from. Maybe nowhere. Maybe they exist because Pēteris and I legislate them into existence. We visit each other in a graveyard at midnight in the middle of winter and agree to live for each other, and when the miraculous taxi appears around the bend in the road, we have caused it to come. We have planted the woods, slicked the headstones with ice, covered the ground with snow. It's our world—ours alone. You all, you go create your own.

***

Pēteris gave me a pineapple to take on the plane from Moscow to Leningrad; then he met me in Riga. A tip for travelers: See that your coat has a loop in the collar, for coatrack hooks. You will keep a lot of inexplicable anger from being directed at you.

In Riga, I heard his music for the first time. We went to the cemetery and he gave me his watch. I went to the water's edge, knowing that Stockholm lay to the west, Finland to the north, jewels, but neither prettier than Riga.

***

My puppy had become my parents'; back in New York, I found a job writing a textbook analyzing Jewish morality tales. I read the Torah, the Talmud, the Midrash, Hasidic folklore. Pēteris would call me up now and then.

And for weeks, I've been trying to call him, unsuccessfully. I don't know why I'm not getting through. It could be my paranoia is no longer neurotic but an accurate reflection of the world I'm inhabiting.

I become depressed, not hearing from Pēteris; I feel anxious, never knowing whether any given letter will be the last to get through. I drink too much, though never inappropriately, and so far I am a good drunk, cheerful and self-sufficient. But there's a terrible ache in my heart, and no scenery short of Soviet scenery can palliate it. One day, some friends and I take a drive to the Pacific Ocean. It's a considerable distance, through lovely wooded country, along a highway. Logging trucks slam past us from the opposite direction every few minutes. We stop to eat sandwiches off a picnic bench and one of the children, Melissa, discovers a miniature rain forest atop a tree

stump—ferns, mold, moss, everything you need to make a
forest is there, made fine. Getting back into the van, we
travel on up to La Push, a corruption of La Bôuche, "the
mouth." The Indians live in a little cluster of shacks; we
drive through the settlement to the ocean—and there it is,
the first time I have seen it. Wearing Melissa's boots and
Hali's windbreaker (I came dressed as an Easterner), I
climb over a pile of very large logs and flat rocks.

My friends must know what I'm thinking, and I rather
wish they didn't. For the same reason, I haven't quoted
from Pēteris's letters herein. Certain feelings are
necessarily enacted privately, since public display falsifies
their very nature, making them melodramatic. My friends
must know I'm thinking about Pēteris, but they don't
know what exactly, or how; they don't know how I feel
about him, how angry I am at the corrosive ideologies that
burn away our earth. (Let's have a Platonic republic; you
be the cobbler, and I'll be a philosopher-king.)

Nor can they know how unexpectedly elated I become,
looking out over the ocean. If only I could walk on water,
the rest would be easy—hopping a freight car on the
Trans-Siberian Express through Skovorodino and
Irkutsk.[4] Something sings in my heart; I have a canary in
my rib cage, and he sings and sings. There's salt on the air,
water in my boot, and music everywhere. Sound is pure
structure, the plan underlying this liberality of existential
stuff, swelling. Three dark rocks rise out of the sea, wet as
seals; under a gray sky, the water is as green as grass.
When a wave begins to break, foam forms first at the outer

---

4 The forest, the taiga, gleams; drops of light fall on birch and
pine like coins into a church's collection plate on Easter,
plentifully.

points and rolls down the wave's length like a prairie catching fire, white fire. The improbable uplifts me, and I know that's why Pēteris loves me: We skirt the edges of absurdity, bringing into being something so unlikely as lasting love. Power and danger, these are enrapturing, as the Apostles found, not to mention Lenin, and they don't preclude hope of a peaceful reunion. The trick is to shed your soul on the beach like a snakeskin; in that profoundly bare condition, you will be able to tread water like ground, the continental shelf will emerge to support you. Amazingly, the farther out you go, the wider your world becomes; your perspective expands, and forsaking de facto being, you achieve the infinite dimensions of the imagination. All things glow; seaweed, clouds, fish are radiant when beheld. The third eye is a tiny Christ nailed to a tiny cross on your forehead, right between the other two.

***

The wind caresses my face like a hand and I remember kissing Pēteris in the cab. I like to kiss, preliminarily or otherwise, and maybe tonight I'll get drunk back at the fort and find somebody else who likes it too. Pēteris knows perfectly well that the live body thrusts and receives and that, as sound is structure, all content is touch. It's getting cold up here, my feet are wet, the kids are hungry, my friends have seen the Pacific before. I drop a pebble into my pocket for a souvenir. I don't feel let down; on the contrary, a voice tells me that, having come so far, from here on I can only come ever closer to the worker whose ambition matches mine, to give song to the earth and its inhabitants, speech to the evolving marsh, sound to rock, soil, and root. Pēteris's music raises me into air, like Pan

Am. Leaving Europe, I looked out the window, seeing the
red land, the blue-white water flashing like diamonds. A
different ocean, the same one world. I turn back from
here, thinking what I thought when I turned back from the
ascending window then, what Pēteris would say, It's from
reality that the winged horses take off.

THE WOMAN WHO

She was my mirror image. I was closer to her than anyone, closer than even a man might be. I used to go with her everywhere, down Sixth Avenue to the bar called The Ninth Circle, up and down Eighth Street on Sunday afternoon to look in the windows and to look at the people looking in the windows or looking at us looking at them. She said it was like walking down an open-ended hallway lined with rows of mirrors reflecting themselves into an infinite regression. She could claim an acuity of analogy, but on the other hand, I kept my eyes open. I saw that when she said this, her eyes sparkled too brilliantly. Her throat tensed and I could see the pulse beating at the base of it even in the hot sun blinding my glasses with glare.

She took off her glasses for a minute to blow the dust from the lenses. An abbreviated storm of breath escaped between her lips. I suggested that she stop for a minute, lean against the storefront and catch her breath. I dug a crumpled tissue from the rubble of my purse, spat on it, and pressed it to her temples. That certainly helped, but she smiled and said (as she always did) that she *always* felt fine. I knew better. She was too thin and growing thinner every day. I wondered if the walks, which in the beginning I had thought would help her grow stronger, were working against us.

"Let's go home," I said, but she shook her head no. She said there was plenty of time to go to the park before we went home, and there would be plenty of time left to take a nap before Dennis arrived. I confess to having given in; I gave in frequently. No matter how hard I tried to put into words my feeling that time was running out, feelings couldn't compete with the facts she argued with. Besides, I didn't want to frighten her about herself any more than she already had been frightened. I could see her body contract under the pressure of space and knew what courage it took to make that journey (for her, it was a journey) east on Eighth across MacDougal and to the right down Fifth to Washington Square.

The pseudo-European arch, the pseudo-entrance, was the closest she would ever come to crossing an ocean— that and the Impressionists in the Metropolitan Museum. It bloomed in the sun like a stone flower; from a distance, even the texture seemed slick like the petals of a flower. Surely this was a victory: a translation of the inorganic into biology that never failed to elicit her admiration. I too had successfully wooed her awe with tales of far-off places that I had photographed.

It was the Sunday before Memorial Day, and the park seemed oddly empty. A group of young men (as she referred to them) were playing volleyball. There were kids, dogs, trees, one or two guitar players. A dark young man sprawled on the grass, his shirt open to the waist, his head lolling as if his neck could no longer support it. But the hipper elements were missing, had hied themselves off to Fire Island and the Hamptons for the holiday weekend. Among those of us who remained, she was conspicuous in her long skirt and muslin blouse. The drawstring at the scoop of the blouse was loose, but hardly worth pointing out. She would laugh and say what did it matter since she had no cleavage; then even so she'd fuss with it. I knew that she thought she was not pretty enough. We were not free women. I had grown up in the South and was still guilty of a more or less mannered mind, if no longer prone to stylized postures. She, conversely, lost no time locating a stage where she might be seen.

Seating herself on a ledge within range of the volleyball court, she pretended to observe what I was doing but not to acknowledge the calm, the cool, with which I put my philosophy into action. I took the long lens, my secondhand Tamron, from its case and attached it to my camera, a new Nikon. I'd learned enough with my old Pentax to go on to something else. My philosophy was that if there were men to be met, they would make themselves known only if I presented an aspect of myself that hinted at others attractively recessed, therefore promising an acquaintanceship of some depth.

She disagreed. She felt men were fatally susceptible to female beauty (that was the way she talked) and even if they could be cured, which she doubted, it was only by catching and conquering the disease. Smiling a bit as she said this, she mocked herself more than she mocked the men. I was afraid she was doing what all single-minded men and women are wont to do: building one bridge which could easily snap in a high wind. I felt she was suspending herself between life and love. And I refuted her strategy by shoring my own gaps with pleasures and disciplines—my camera—to ensure an exit when the time came (for I knew time was running out) to make my getaway from the Land of Loss. In any case, that is what I theorized as I assembled my camera, hiked my draggy India-print skirt up between my knees, and started shooting the kids and the dogs in the park.

"Take my picture, please, lady," the kid said. He was small, smaller than he should have been for his age, I guessed. I didn't like his peremptory tone. "I don't care," I said, "for your peremptory tone of voice." I moved backward on my seat as far as the ledge would allow. He was too close for the lens I was using.

"You don't know how to take pictures nohow," he said, spoiling for a fight.

I was aware of a frown hovering over my roommate's face. It came to rest, and she half turned toward the volleyball game. She disliked scenes. Already a six-year-old red-haired girl I'd been shooting was speaking to the intruder. "*You* don't know *nothing*," she said. "Good grief."

"I do too—" He got down from his bike but had to move farther away for me to get the framing right. "I'm Batman," he yelled. Winging his arms, he flew into her face and stuck out his tongue.

She was tough. "Boys don't know nothing."

The others formed a semicircle and I felt we were in a theater.

"Move back." I was authoritative and they moved back. The girl and the boy stared at each other. "If you're Batman," I said, coming between them with my peaceable talk, "where is your cape?"

"Ha, ha," the girl cried.

"My cape," he answered, squaring his chin smack in my line of sight, "is in the wash. It got dirty when I beat up on my sister."

I clicked the shutter.

I didn't know how the redhead could fail to love him after that—the bluster, the sass so quickly thought of. I thought any pint-sized ball-breaker would shuffle her allegiances to adore a man who stood firm. But the girl said, "Who does the wash? Your fat mother, ain't it."

"My mother ain't fat."

"She is too! Fat like a pig."

"My mother," he said, "is prettier than you."

The girl's face bunched up like a fist. Crying, "*Fat like a pig! The fattest pig in the world!*" she ran to the other side of the park. The boy slowly mounted his bike and rode off in the opposite direction. The kids dispersed. I put my camera away. "Let's go home," I said again.

She said something then about the little girl's being a poor little girl, because of what the boy had said. That made me angry, because she made everything come back to looks. She always did. "You mean yourself, don't you," I shouted, jumping down from the ledge. "No one came over to talk to you. Well, they didn't talk to me either but at least I got some pictures taken and that's worth something to *me*." I watched her gathering herself together as I spoke. We knew each other too well. "We can't afford to be sentimental about children," I said, trying to reshape and soften my criticism. "It's too dangerous for us." Because we were single and in our thirties. On the way home she had a coughing fit, and as soon as we got in I made her take a nap.

***

There was an owl on our wall: a poster of orange and dark brown. The eyes, set close together, formed an inverted triangle with the beak. The poster bespoke a certain penetration that gave her the willies, but I had a yen for the wisdom it represented. She let me keep my poster because I in turn tolerated her mirror. (One made compromises.) She would stand in front of the mirror as long as she could manage and when she grew tired would pull up a stool to apply, carefully, the eye shadow she wore even though it was out of fashion. She said blue made her eyes look bigger—that they were beady without make-up. Every time, she dispensed this information with a matter-of-factness that stripped my sense of self to its tattered underwear. Every time, I said she looked fine either way. It was not *my* approval she sought, because she would go right on making up her face.

I sat at the table under the owl poster and began to put my slides in order.

Looking in the mirror I could see her as she lay on the bed, still wearing the long skirt and the muslin blouse. She rolled over in her sleep, pulled the bedspread up and wrapped it over herself. I asked if she was feeling all right. She was sound asleep despite the movement so I turned away, back to my slides. Then I heard her cry out and I knew she was having a nightmare again.

She said she dreamed she was dreaming, and in her dream of a dream she was sleeping as I fooled with the slides of her in her nightgown, her robe, her draggy skirt and muslin blouse. Now, in all the time we had lived together, I had never taken a picture of her—which was, I thought, to be expected. But I resented the importance she attached to my camera, as if it contained the meaning of our relationship. Once I called her on this and she retreated. Since I didn't want to be the cause of any irremediable rift I didn't mention it again. But I felt all the same that a camera was a camera and not, so help us both, a correspondence.

In the dream, she said, the camera held a secret message. I had placed it in the Russian Embassy to be picked up, but Illya Kuryakin (I smiled at this image of my TV-oriented youth) got there first. He was on holiday, not spying for either side in the Cold War, but out of simple professional curiosity he went to see what the message was, and found, in the camera, a beautiful, tall, reedy, unlit candle. He wanted to take it somewhere where there weren't any authorities so he could look at it in peace and quiet. He tucked it under his shirt, a cylindrical shape at the breast pocket, and walked out of the Embassy, worried that the bulge would attract attention. Strolling as casually as he could, he crossed a wide, cultivated lawn to the concrete sidewalk. He broke into a run. Nobody followed him and before nightfall he found himself in the screened-in upstairs porch of an estate that was shut down while the owners were on vacation. He sat down in a rocker and set the candle on the chair rail, his whole body sinking into the pleasure of unadulterated viewing. Precisely then the owners drove up and discovered him quite by accident. When he ran they took him for a thief and began to shoot. Wounded in the neck, he slipped on the damp edge of the pool and fell in. He would have drowned in his own blood if she hadn't awakened.

"You shouldn't let dreams scare you," I said (not with any real sympathy, because we had been through this before). I figured dreams were less frightening than the way she coughed, or barely touched her meals. She said I was right and went to take a bath. I followed her in. The sleep-sweat stood out all over her skin, so I said she'd better make the bath a cool one. Underwater her legs were slick and white, waxy as an artificial flower, but the hairs brushed by the currents in the tub seemed more plumage than petal. Still, they were not at all like the feathers on the owl in the poster on the wall above the dining table where I catalogued my slides.

***

Dennis rang the doorbell three times in quick succession. He was extravagant in everything. Star student in his class at Virginia Law, he'd turned down considerable offers to work for next to nothing at a nonprofit agency promoting Zero Population Growth.

He announced himself over the intercom. "Women," he said at the door, fixing us with a significant stare, "will yet win control over their own bodies. Even if I have to do it for them!"

"You're drunk, Dennis," I said, my spirits soaring, my chiding voice reflexive.

He aimed a kiss in my direction. For a minute I tightened up, thinking she might feel left out, dismissed with too cavalier a sweep. But with generosity he threw his arms around her. I almost told him to be careful, I could have sworn she'd gotten thinner even since this morning, but it was painfully clear to me how much she appreciated the hug. I knew they'd slept together and I hoped he wasn't going to let her down. Dennis and I had been buddies before either of us had moved north, and I knew he wasn't the most stable of souls. But he was fun, and when he extended an elbow and jokingly asked me to "step on out," I hesitated before saying no. I tried never to go where I wasn't sure I was wanted, but he could tell I wanted to go. "Oh, come on, Lindy," he said, "you don't want to stay home on a holiday."

"The holiday isn't until tomorrow," I said.

"Everybody stays in and sleeps late on holidays," he reasoned; "it's the *eve* you want to celebrate." Quick on the uptake.

I was still making up my mind.

"Think of Christmas," he said, "think of New Year's!"

In his vehemence the wisps of yellow hair he combed forward flew back, exposing his prematurely balding pate. I laughed and got ready to say no again, when out of the corner of my own eye I noticed a blue-lidded one just waiting to blink me out of the picture. "Okay," I said. Brightly. "We must all celebrate the eve of Memorial Day!" he said. We rode down in the elevator. Marching at his side down Sixth Avenue past the A&P and the drugstore, I raised my voice. "Memorial Day is rather special. It's a day for remembering people who've done you a service." There was no echo from his other side, but he had his hand on her neck. I supposed she was not so sad or so mad if she was liking Dennis and breathing the cooled-off air of the night.

There wasn't a cloud in the sky, all the stars strung out against a clear black depth of field. She said the stars looked anguished, as though they'd been abandoned by the sun. "Shall we should keep the stars *company*?" I asked. Dennis ignored my sarcasm and leapt at the idea. "We'll have a picnic on my roof," he said. She speedily seconded the suggestion. I worried she might catch cold, but I found myself in the deli helping her choose cheese and bread and olives and paper napkins while Dennis stopped next door to pick up some white wine and plastic cups. His office was in a landmark building on Patchin Place, a secret, cunning alleyway on Tenth between The Americas and Greenwich.

As soon as we entered through the wrought-iron gate, I felt we were in a different country. Warm light from conscientiously, comfortably decorated living rooms filtered out to the alley, but the iron door behind us shut out the street sounds you learn to rely on in New York. There were trees, too, glowing blue-black in the electric light, and the wind fanned their leaves with a subtle whirring noise. We held the groceries while Dennis unlocked his door, trailed him up a carpeted staircase past thousands of law books, past ersatz living quarters where he and his partners could play poker or take a breather from difficult cases without precedent, and entered the top room. It was bare except for wall-to-wall carpeting, a desk, a lamp, a telephone, and a silky, silvery, expensive goat rug on top of the carpet.

Wrapping the rug around his shoulders, Dennis led the way through the window onto the fire escape, with me picking up the rear. She stopped on the landing to look down and I followed her gaze four flights down to the courtyard at the bottom. At the top of the ladder Dennis was saying, "Don't look down and you'll be all right." She gripped the ladder and started up but then said her shoes, rubber-soled, would slip. He told her to take them off. Barefoot then to the top, long, cotton skirt billowing behind her in the breeze, she swelled and rose, a woman in eternal emergence. I poked my head over the roof and Dennis hauled me up.

She said her feet were cold and of course he whipped the rug from his shoulders to spread before her like a cape of chivalry. When I suggested she put her shoes back on, she said the rug felt lovely, she could feel its silkiness all the way from the periphery of her skin to the very bones of her body. Dennis said he knew what she meant and took off his shoes. Then she took off her sweater, exposing the blouse that failed to expose anything more significant than the too-prominent collarbone, the crescent framed by the scoop of muslin. Annoyed, I laid out the food and poured the wine. "Liberation," he said, as I filled his glass; "this is that I like about it."

"The service, you mean?" I poured a tiny bit of the wine on his bare toes, and then got some on his shirt when I turned the bottle back upright. He cursed and took his shirt off. "Why don't you go right ahead and strip," I said. He complimented me for all the terrific ideas I was having tonight. But I'd only meant to be sarcastic, and I could see by the light of our friends the stars that whatever I said exacted a price. She pretended to be amused by Dennis. I could tell she was holding her breath, sensed the momentary cessation of breathing. We had spread out the food and were lying on our sides like Romans to eat it. Dennis, half-crocked to begin with, gulped his wine and shed the rest of his clothes. He had round shoulders, long legs, sparse hair. He said freedom was beautiful. I asked him what he would do if someone reported him to the police.

"Relax," he said. "I do this all the time." He smiled. "Alone, of course."

"Of course."

"Try it," he said. "You'll like it."

"It's cold."

He said he'd keep me warm; it was the only proper thing to say under the circumstances. I didn't want to be a poor sport. "*I'm* not an exhibitionist," I said. He asked me what my fantasies *were*. I had no idea what to say, and my glance fell on the rug. "Goats," I said.

He rammed his head into my long skirt, butting between my legs, taking the cloth in his mouth, tugging. "Don't talk with your mouth full," I said.

"Goats will eat anything."

I laughed. "Thanks a lot!" I was high and stepped out of my skirt. "What do you dream about? What do you daydream about?"

He rocked back on his haunches, considering. "A threesome might do it for me."

I asked what a threesome could do. Clouds were now scudding across the stars. The play of light and dark on his face was plainly devil's play, baring the shape of skull, the forward-thrusting, goatish jaw, slanted eyes, something of horn in the shape of the ear.

"This is absurd," I said, and sat down on the rug. Our legs were touching. I could tell she wanted to move away from me toward him, but he said, "We love each other, don't we? In the best sense?" and compassed us in his grip.

"You bet," I said, none too seriously. She was beaming. Beatific. But the legs betrayed her: They were trembling. She said she couldn't help it, she'd been cold all her life, but she believed in brother- and sisterhood. I asked Dennis what having two women would accomplish. He seemed bewildered, as though he'd forgotten. Then he ran his thumb down my cheek, a gesture I cautioned myself to suspect, and said he couldn't help it, he was by nature expansive.

She said she understood, she too felt the urge to expand. I was surprised at so bald-faced a lie till I realized she was bound to say exactly that. Compliance was a form of charity, the honeyed yea-saying a way to enact her will. Yet, I noted, she had kept her blouse on. Her arms crisscrossed her breasts to shield them from the elements, and I was sure Dennis was one of the elements. Then I said, "Suppose you were into a thing like that, a threesome, and it freaked somebody's head out, because wouldn't the two women have to have sex with each other?"

"Only if they wanted to. Think how beautiful it must be."

He rubbed his cheeks against the rug. "It would be such a natural thing, an effortless expression of—of—Lord, I'm tired of feeling *obligated*. It would be free."

He would want us to hold hands. I didn't want to hold hands. I was afraid if I held hands I would never get loose. Besides, it would be the same as making love to myself, and what was special about that?

"I don't think so," I said. "You'd really have to convince me first."

"Convince!" he snorted. As if I'd said something stupid, said (to borrow her idiom) a dirty word.

"What?" I said. "What did I say?"

"Jesus, Lindy, fantasies are not about being *convinced.*"

"Maybe they are for me," I said. And for her: I knew that she had been hurt by his suggestion of a threesome. As if she were insufficient or inadequate.

"What's the use. For crying out loud, what's the use." He yanked his arms away, turned on his side. "What's the mother use," he mumbled.

"Are you going to sleep?"

He *was* asleep. I paced the roof, trying to think of something to do. "What's the use," I muttered. I peered out over the alley. The living-room lights were off. It looked as though it might rain, and I wished it would, wished it would rain torrents on that white body, gleaming like a beached, bleached bone against the rug and black tar paper. What did he mean, *convince.* It was Dennis who slept, safely removed from sex and liberation, not I. It was I, not Dennis Duval Duplessis Mullins, who prowled this roof, taking pictures in my mind's eye.

As I looked at the sky, it occurred to me that time was raining, pouring from the stars through recently arrived, small clouds into my hands, slipping through my hands onto the roof and splattering into the alley in drops and dribbling away to nothing. I was getting old, older, old. I was tired and lay down to sleep, tugging Dennis' left arm from behind his neck to lay my head on. I fell asleep, but in the middle of the night I heard her cough and opened my eyes and closed them again and heard her cough again.

In the morning I heard whispering. "Let's go for a bike ride," he said. She said it was too early. He said, "I think a bike ride would be very healthful, I feel full of energy." She suggested he direct some of that energy toward her. I wanted to shut out the sound of her voice, but that timid whisper commanded my audience. I couldn't very well say, *This is my head; this is my territory, keep your humiliations on your side of the fence.* He said, penitent now, "I'm sorry, it just doesn't seem to be that kind of energy, does it." She said she wished she knew why. She asked why he didn't want to make love to her. He said, as a barrister might, "Sex isn't something a person can legislate. You make me feel I'm supposed to feel something, like I owe it to you. I don't want to be in debt to you; I don't want to owe anybody anything." She was persistent. Did that mean he never wanted to make love to her again? "How can I know," he asked, irritable, "how I'll feel tomorrow? I don't think I'll want to." She asked why not. He said, twisting as if he were bound by ropes and had to work himself free, "I have my—prejudices, my physical prejudices. Like everyone else. It's nothing personal." I closed my eyes but felt him turn toward her and cover her face with his hands. "What I like about you," he said, "is, you have character. You know?" She didn't answer. "You know what I mean?" he said.

I stirred, noisily, clumsily, being casual, dissembling anger, but how could I help being angry at her for letting him talk to her like that. "The sun is shining," I said. "It's going to be another one."

"Another what?"

"Another hot day," I said. His face looked young in the bright sunshine, the high dome of his forehead newly hatched. "Sometimes, Dennis," I said, "I think you're chicken." Though I didn't say it, I really thought he looked like a fetus, perfectly formed and all-too-successfully aborted.

"Don't pull that stuff on me," he said.

"You can say those things to me—" I began, wanting to tell him he had no right to say them to her, *I* was the one with character, only a fool could mix us up. What had he done!

"I'm only being truthful!" he shouted, so loud I feared he would wake the neighbors. He caught himself and lowered his voice. "I'm only being honest about my feelings. I thought," he said, sighing, "we were good enough friends that we could be truthful with each other. I guess I was wrong."

"I guess you were," I agreed.

"I guess," he said, "the woman doesn't exist who likes to hear the truth."

"I guess not." I twisted my skirt at the waistband until it was on right.

"What are you doing?"

"Getting ready to go home."

"It's too early."

I didn't think so. The remains of the night were haunting us, the untouched cheese, the empty wine bottles, the bread a feast for a swarm of red ants. It looked late to me, very late. I waited while she put her shoes on, and it seemed she took a very long time. I could tell she was weary. I felt I had to force her to put her shoes on. I picked up her sweater and tied the sleeves around my neck.

"I'll call," he said.

I nodded and we started to leave.

"Wait a minute," he said. I turned. He was still cross-legged on the rug. He was tapping his index finger against his jaw. "Aren't you going to kiss me good-bye?"

I was surprised. He said, "We *are* friends, old ones, whether you like it or not." As I shook my head no, she walked toward him, knelt down and kissed the side of his face.

I imagined he heard the iron gate bang behind us as we, falling silent, went out onto the street and turned toward Sixth Avenue. "Well," I said, searching for something. I would have said, *That was a bummer*, or *So much for Dennis*, or something on that order, but I didn't dare.

Then I did dare. "I didn't know you were capable of prostituting yourself," I said, the words telling me I was still angry. I needed to be sure she knew it. "You throw yourself at them. Every single time. You say, Take me, I'm yours. I'm yours for the taking. You'd just lie right down and let them walk all over you, wouldn't you. Wouldn't you!"

She flinched but held her tongue. We turned up Sixth Avenue. The street was empty, it was too early, people stayed in and slept on holidays. Side by side we walked while I talked. Then she said dignity was all in how you looked at it. It was nobler to go on accepting people at face value, giving them what they asked for. If you held back you had no right expecting to receive in return.

We had stopped in front of the A&P. On the other side of the plate glass window were cartons of soft drinks, bags of charcoal, potted begonias, but they were nothing to me. I spoke to her reflection. The shadow had creased in the folds of her eyelids, the powder vanished during the night. The skin looked grainy, like a newspaper photo, like a rock. This was an aspect I'd never noticed: the hardness.

"So when things go wrong, you can say it wasn't *your* fault, *you* were only trying to please, *you* didn't mean to hurt anybody. Miss High-and-Mighty! Miss Good-and-True! Miss Holier-than-Thou!" Beneath the blouse, her thin shoulders swayed like the first leaves of summer in a windstorm. I thought she would fly away and I wanted to pin her to the ground. "You think I should admire your silence, your forbearance, your difference from the rest of the world. Well, maybe I don't like what's different any more than the rest of the world does. Maybe I don't think just because you're special you're beautiful. Maybe I don't think you're special!" I stopped. I didn't want to believe I'd gone too far.

She turned on me those small brown eyes in painted hoods. The curve of chin escaped into the curve of neck and torso and limb and then she walked away. The sun shone down more brightly, a bright beam, a spotlight focused on her thin body, the blouse, the India-print skirt. Before my eyes she grew smaller and thinner, moving away from me, heading east, not once glancing back. The margin between body and light narrowed, blurring until the light radiating from hair and hem converged in my own eye. She turned a corner and was gone.

No, I didn't believe it. She would go to the park for a while and then come back. I stood on the corner in front of the barred and barricaded newsstand, but she didn't reappear. Finally I pulled myself together and went home. I thought about calling my friends—"Have you seen the woman who was not pretty enough?" I would ask—but my friends would be disturbed and not understand. In the evening I went out to look for her, but she wasn't anywhere—only the kids from the New School, the window cleaners in the A&P, the shuffling regulars and irregulars in the Blimpies. At the end of Sixth Avenue, in the far distance, the twin towers of the World Trade Center glimmered in perilous balance.

I went to Eighth Street, to Washington Square, to the arch, but she wasn't there. And looked behind trees and around corners, but she was never there.

I looked everywhere I could think of.

It's been almost five months now, going on half a year, and I'm thinking of moving, maybe even back south, just so her absence from this room won't crowd me so. I know there are those who, hearing our story, would say I'm better off without her, leave well enough alone, she's probably happily shacked up with some half-baked poet, but after you get used to living with someone, it's hard to adapt. And you tell me what poet is going to have the sense to take care of that cough. She could be dead by now! Depending on a poet!

I could say how terribly alone I sometimes imagine I am, but I don't know why I should have to. She must have known how lonely I would be! After all, we were closer than anyone. It's a rotten trick she played on me, for how was I to know she would do just what she did when I said what I said? Or that I would miss her so or become so everlastingly bored talking to an empty room. When it's perfectly dark, and I can be sure no one else is listening but I want to think she may be, I go outside and call her name. And then I'm apt to feel foolish, or even—let us be frank—thoroughly put out. She always needed so much looking after.

AN AMERICAN ARCADY (NOTES)

EPIGRAPH. This poem by William Blake from his book *For the Sexes: The Gates of Paradise*:

> Truly, My Satan, thou art but a Dunce,
> And dost not know the Garment from the Man.
> Every Harlot was a Virgin once,
> Nor can'st thou ever change Kate into Nan.
>
> Tho' thou art Worship'd by the Names Divine
> Of Jesus & Jehovah, thou art still
> The Son of Morn in weary Night's decline,
> The lost Traveller's Dream under the Hill.

***

WHERE IT OPENS. On German School Road, because the world as we know it was taught to be what it is by Germany. This holds true even for the Soviet Union, as, without Hitler, at least a few of the Socialist Republics, not to mention East Europe, might have been able to steer clear of Stalin—and his successors. Does it hold for China? But is China part of the world as we know it?

***

THE THEME. *Et in Arcadia ego.*

***

THE BACKGROUND. A white stucco house sits back from the road—German School Road. Sometimes the house dissolves into a morning mist, glimmering like a ghost house briefly before vanishing. The climbing sun brings it forward again, knocking against cement, sand and lime, clarifying. If being is texture, this simple stucco house exists, palpably, and as C. S. Peirce might have said, brutally. As the day lengthens, shadows pour into the street like a black river.

I remember watching this surging night tide from the dormer window of my attic room.

***

FROM THE MARGIN. Not all being is textured, of course. There are dreams, memories, and imaginary numbers, among other things. These can be considered blueprints for being. They are directions for the might-be or the might-have-been, or even for what was. Such modes of being may be called texts.

***

BACKGROUND (cont'd). Next door, Elizabeth and Joseph Allen rehearse string quartets with Wechsberg and Wüslich, from the Richmond Professional Institute, where Joseph Allen taught violin and theory. He was on the faculty for twenty-five years. Even long before that, once upon a time, Elizabeth was his student, a beautiful, tall girl who lived in a swamp, swam in the Gulf, and ultimately accomplished the brusque attitudes of the world but without ever quite managing to shake the sense of some lost—not happiness, exactly—but some lost sufficiency, a being-alone that was like having the whole world to yourself. She had been a young woman who fell in love with her teacher, and now here they both were, in their sixties.

There is a footstool between them, Elizabeth and Joseph, for holding cigarettes and Cokes. A soft circle of light from the floor lamp in the center shines equitably on all four music stands, and attached to each music stand is a twist of wire that holds pencils. A brown-and-white dog sleeps near the crewel-covered footstool.

Upstairs, James Robert Allen speed-reads detective novels from his father's shelf, keeps a diary that he refers to as a log, and seeks to keep his drinking subtle.

His sister, Kathryn Partridge Allen, occupies the room across the hall; she is seated at her desk, writing, writing about a character named Lindy Applewhite, her character of the moment. Kathryn has the window open, and the chill air makes her feel alive and quick, like a new twig in a loud wind.

Kathryn is *my* character. I allow her to be more resilient than I am, less conventional, less easily bollixed, less mindful of other people in good ways and in bad. She writes fiction, finding fiction more interesting than fact (or what she assumes is fact), but she earns her living doing odd jobs for publishers, or on occasion selling magazines over the telephone under a false name. You never know who could be on the other end of the line.

Kathryn's defining characteristic is that through her fiction she is able to entertain herself with her own traumas, but for this reward, a price is exacted. Writers write, and that creates consequences. Kathryn, whom I devised, in turn created Melinda, a/k/a Lindy, who isn't my alter ego but hers. Unlike either of them, I, Nan, am real. (I insist on that, on my reality, though I wouldn't go to war or fight a duel over it. Maybe I wouldn't even insist on it.)

I know my place in my own story, and my role in the yet more inclusive story that began with the Word. A dramatic conflict lifts the fallen hickory leaves, some unpredictable conclusion drifts over the dark pavement like fog. Down the street, the Spooner house is silent—there are children there, asleep—and in the Applewhite house, Lindy and her father talk idly for a few minutes before retiring to their rooms. Lindy looks over her day's photographs; her father looks over his notes—he's just initiated a likely experiment at the lab. A light goes out; a light goes out.

How do Lindy and Kathryn live in the same neighborhood? How do Kathryn and I live in the same neighborhood? Do I live in the world with God?

Does God exist? Sometimes.

In February, snow covers the ground, blue-white under a full moon. Its crust shines. Elizabeth Allen throws her camel's-hair coat on over her pajama top and underpants, puts on galoshes, and walks the dog. He tugs like crazy, excited by the cold weather. She is abstracted (why?) and lets the leash slip, but the leash wasn't really necessary in the first place. It was Elizabeth's excuse for getting out of the house alone.

***

It is night now, but for the same reason—to be alone—Elizabeth also rises earlier than anyone else, using the time not to brood but to clip recipes, write letters, read. But sometimes she broods. She hears Jimmy getting up overhead; alcohol interferes with the sleep mechanism, and her son is an insomniac, but he won't come down yet, knowing she needs her private time. She waits in the kitchen. She hears Joe's light switch go on, knows he will read, but not speed-read, detective novels until daybreak. She hears Kathryn tiptoe down the hall to the bathroom. It's three-thirty in the morning and everyone is wide awake; the whole house is breathing, but no one dares to intrude on anyone else. Elizabeth waits. Something is about to happen. The tension flutters around her heart like a light bug around a lamp.

***

CHARACTERS. The lawyer, Bob Braumiller, has a woman friend in his bed. She wears Casaque perfume—he asked—and snores delicately. He sneaks downstairs to write a note to his daughter, away at school. In the silver frame next to the marble pen-and-ink stand, he can see his daughter's pretty face, dark hair windblown across her left cheek, and on the glass over her face, like a double exposure, his own crew-cut reflection looking angry and trapped.

He lets his eyes wander. From the rec room window, he sees that the Dawsons are still up. Or one of them, anyway. Probably Dick.

***

About any married couple, he thinks, it is useful to know which one goes to bed first.

***

PROFILE OF RICHARD DAWSON. Tall. Too thin. Mackintosh in wet weather. Diffident, kindly. Tolerant. A romantic manqué. A businessman. Owns his own firm. At his core, he is dead serious. His jokes make other people slightly uncomfortable, as if they were suffering from heartburn or had been standing too long in one place. There's nothing wrong with the jokes, it's the way he tells them. He knows this about himself, knows he is never his real self except when he is with his mistress, in her arms, accepted by her. Away from her, he lives on anxiety: One reason he stays with his wife, Sonja, is that she feeds his sense of impending doom. Absorbing from her daily the quiet, restrained, almost furtive tremor of excitement in her soul, a *measured* dread, that quantification of the Unknown being what he seeks and values in marriage. On the night in question, his wife is staring across the table at him as if some message has been written on his face which he will never be able to read.

**

LINES. A cold rain tilting through pine needles and bare dogwood branches. The old woman's head thrust pugnaciously forward over a bin of cantaloupes. The universe seeping outward through space like a gigantic stain on the fabric of nonbeing.

**

CHARACTERS (cont'd). When Herb Szazy by way of medical advice suggested a hobby, Dick Dawson became an astronomy buff, and in warm, dry weather, when grass is as brittle as kindling, he may now be seen lying on his back outdoors, learning the stars by name. He is building a small dome to house his telescope.

In the new age, we will all have to know our way around the sky. Hang around on the earth too long and you could run into laser beams from strategic satellites, nerve gas, nuclear terrorism.

In fact, with these possibilities in mind, Garth Ferguson, when he was a teenager, used to keep an Eveready battery, distilled water, and twenty cans of black-eyed peas under his bed, but unlike Dick Dawson, as he grew older, he became increasingly dissatisfied with the view from Virginia. He fell into a kind of protracted discontent. His parents still live in the house on the other side of Chabasinski's park.

**

All of the people here assume greater or lesser ontological density depending on whose world they move in, mine, Kathryn's, or Lindy Applewhite's.

This seems to me to be in the general scheme of things, no matter what psychological Ptolemaicism we hanker after or are encouraged to believe we might, at least in America, reclaim. I know, for example, that I move in a number of worlds but exist most nearly completely in one, whose Maker I love. Who is, however, an inveterate rewriter, erasing whole species for the sake of a single topic sentence. The Maker (and Unmaker) of makers. Though we can never know for sure what quality of opacity God prescribes for any of us, it's obviously necessarily more substantial than in succeeding refractive realms. The question is one of degree: *To what power of the imagination are we raised, short of the nth?*

The point is, I suppose, that each of us is an event, whether more or less real. *I* am an event. I can be located in space-time, and my texture is not disagreeable. I have pretty hair and great legs, and my face, while not all I might want it to be, is real enough to register hope and loss.

One more thing I'm sure of: The farther from yourself you travel, the more World comes into View.

You ride the train past your stations, leave the historical self behind, and move into newness. Christ said, He that would find his life must lose his life.

So here's my Being—I give it to you (the unnamed Reader). My body's yours; enjoy it. My mind is yours; don't let it get you down. My soul is full of longing—but only sometimes.

***

THE NOISE. I hear a noise and go to investigate. It is autumn now. I wear an outsized dark-green knitted sweater, blue jeans and boots. The noise eludes me. I sit on a wooden bench. The noise again!

Jimmy Allen joins me, his body slung in its usual defensive posture. "Sit for a while," I say, wanting to put him at ease. "Aren't you cold?"

He is wearing a corduroy jacket that can't be very warm.

"I'm fine," he says.

"It's started getting cold at night."

He doesn't answer; he is smoking a cigarette.

"When are you headed back?"

He lives in New York, and is down here only long enough to recuperate from a divorce. Divorce runs in their family, like low blood pressure.

"I don't know. Another month maybe."

"What have you been doing with yourself?" I am being polite.

"Nothing much. Reading detective novels."

"I'm a science-fiction fan, myself."

"I thought so. You're the type."

I resent that. His tone is aggressive: He attacks with his voice, counters with his body, shoulders hunched. "And what is that supposed to mean?" I say.

"It doesn't mean anything. People divide into two groups, those who read detective novels and those who read science fiction."

It was not unlike the division between rationalists and empiricists.

"Science fiction is popular metaphysics," I say. Pleased with myself.

He nods and flicks his cigarette into the forsythia and lilac cave, a large flowery shell with a dirt floor where Trudy and Pug Spooner like to play house. Off in the opposite direction is Mr. Dawson's backyard telescope.

"Don't look now," Jimmy says, "but my inestimable sister is on her way over."

Actually, I like Kathryn; she's tough, she has a hard-nosed nonchalance I would have liked for myself; all she lacks is a sense of peace. But I know that at this point Jim desires peace and simplicity above anything else, and he isn't likely to get them from her. Sympathetically, I touch his coat sleeve and then his hand. It breaks the spell, and he becomes mere air. I am gazing on illusion. Prickly wind blows my hair in my face, and Kathryn becomes a tall tree, rooted.

***

FROM THE MARGIN. Everyone pays a tax on the currency of the heart. This is something we know but don't believe.

***

DESCRIPTIVE PASSAGE (*late afternoon*). The rain had more or less stopped, and the clouds looked washed out. The sky was a little lighter now, the leaves on the trees yellow and green, those that had fallen already red. Water dripped down the window from overhanging roof tiles. In a literary mood, you might imagine that if you mated Freud and Kafka, you'd get this changing of the seasons: the primal metamorphosis. (Note: Avoid elaborate jokes.)

***

PROFILE OF SONIA DAWSON. Redhead. Slightly sway-backed. Regretful. Wide-eyed. Mother of one son. Now forty-one and grieving over lost time more than she ever had over lost love, though she would never have said she was a good sport about *that*, exactly. Maiden name Björnson. From Minnesota. Her mother, back home in Minnesota, drives a pickup truck to the grocery store in Cottonwood on Saturdays. Sonja's father lost his hand in a threshing machine and when he ate he kept his claw in his lap. They looked like any other American family eating dinner, until you looked under the table.

***

THE TIME. Sometimes earlier, sometimes later. Not necessarily in that order.

***

SYMBOLS. Cymbals for symbols. When I think of Christ on the cross, I hear sublime music, and it bothers me because I think that when he died, every pleasurable and exalted feeling must also have died. I am sure an extraordinary silence seized the earth, hushing even birds.

***

SCENES. Here, and there. It depends on the time, or vice versa.

Consider in this connection: our lust for the promised land, a place shed of all contingency, where the granaries are forever full, the highways never come to an end, and divorce is a game of musical chairs in which no one is ever left standing up.

So what if these hopes are naïve. Back of them lies the memory of a world closed and guarded by cherubim, and a flaming sword which turns every way. Ahead lies the other tree, the one that is sprawled against the sheet-metal sky like a parody of Eden. Under the circumstances, a little wishful thinking can't hurt.

***

FROM THE MARGIN. America was to have been the new Jerusalem. The state of Virginia might have been the heavenly kingdom (some Virginians think it is).

***

CHARACTERS (cont'd). In the house on the corner, Lindy Applewhite scribbles poems. She doesn't take them seriously—she takes photography seriously—but they are a release. From what? Her brain is crowded, she hates the cacophony. Still, she is a lonely young woman, having lost her faith, and in lieu of sex or God, doggerel will help her to pass the time.

Is she so passive because she is thrice removed from the prime mover? Aristotle would argue that she is passive because she is not male.

***

FROM THE MARGIN. The void that seduces male philosophers is to women merely familiar. Contrarily, a woman conceives of love as a bringing forth. *Ex nihilo*, text and texture.

***

CHARACTERS (cont'd). Bob Braumiller climbs back into bed, trying not to disturb his woman friend, but he bumps his knee against the frame. He makes a face in the dark. His friend has a moment of fright, sleepily imagining that she is at home in her own bed, being intruded upon by a stranger. "Oh, it's you," she says, recognizing Bob. He wonders who she thought it was. The President?

***

RECAPITULATION. I hear a noise and go to investigate. It is still autumn. Someone in the Allen house is playing a record, the Goldberg Variations. But that is sound, not noise, not the noise I hear. I sit on the bench and listen carefully. Silence.

***

NOTES ON A NOTE (*must stop these musical parallels*). What we strive for until the end of our days is the pure line of the boy soprano.

A lie. Persuaded by the sound of my own words.

***

VARIATIONS ON A THEME. Somewhere far from home you will come in touch with the person who gives meaning to your life. This is not a fashionable thought but it is, unlike the preceding one, true. Meaning is provided from the outside; if meaning is not provided from the outside, you are locked in your own mind, and that is solipsism.

So much for philosophy. The rest of it is, *There is a person you love, and that person is not you.*

He hides in the hills, sleeps in the meadow. He's as patient as water wearing a passage through rock, but his soul is full of longing.

***

FROM THE MARGIN. A promise is a promise. This is something we believe but don't know. (Whoops, there goes the unassailability of tautologies.)

***

That becoming human is an infinitely arduous task, impossible without metaphor and a constant testing of limits, the tender bruising of object by object which bespeaks a world of restraint, creates a world of relation.

***

CHARACTERS (cont'd). When Garth comes home on vacation, during the summer, he sits in the rope-and-board swing behind his house, reading. Or he meditates in his room. "A koan is a question from the Unknown." The sound of one hand clapping—this is a famous koan. A less celebrated koan is, Why is the wind invisible? There are no gimmicky answers here, and Garth knows it. He goes into the kitchen through the back door to fix a tuna fish sandwich and a glass of Kool-Aid. Every time he opens the refrigerator, a blast of cold air dries the sweat on his face. The sun paints the kitchen a deep golden red, glazes the linoleum counter top like lacquer. Garth takes his sandwich and drink into the next room, thinking he might call up a girl he was introduced to last week. Xenia...he can't remember the last name; he'll have to get it from his friend on Monday.

There's Carol Braumiller, of course, but she's too young. Kate Allen is too old.

He flips through a *Sports Illustrated*.

How do I know this? I am there. How do you know I'm not? As Lord Russell asked, How do you know there is not a hippopotamus in the room?

***

DESCRIPTIVE PASSAGE (*late night*). A writer is writing a story by hand at the kitchen table. A small television set at the end of the table is turned to a science-fiction horror film. The scientist's daughter and his handsome young assistant are whispering urgently. The father is a genius gone berserk, the young man equally brilliant but of a corporate mentality, and the girl, of course, pretty but forgettable.

The writer goes to the sink to rinse out a coffee cup; the window over the sink is open. Outside, a high wind punishes the pines, and the rushing noise seems to mingle with the soft voices coming from the television, until the writer is wrapped in a kind of murmuring like a long, strangling scarf around the throat.

There's a superstition that says: If a girl does such-and-such and looks out her window on the stroke of midnight, she will see either her husband-to-be or the way of her death. The girl I heard about saw a white stallion; she broke her neck riding. I don't know what the such-and-such is, and the thing about any ritual that you don't know is that you have to be especially cautious, lest you perform it by accident.

***

RE: PLACE (*Richmond?*). If, as scientists say, everything is moving away from everything else, that can only leave each of us at the center of it all, throbbing with egocentricity. But if everyone else is at the center of it all, we are on the black rim beyond reach, calling, from the margin, "Touch me, touch me!" Howling interminably across interstellar wastes. Not all the heat of a billion burning stars can begin to warm that galactic chill, the lone atom locked in its cubic foot of space. And yet the real world is smaller than the known one—or perhaps the known world is smaller than the real one—and people's lives in it brush and mesh.

***

THE SUBPLOT. There is a party at the Dawsons' to celebrate Richard's winning bid on a government contract. Charcoaled steaks in the backyard. Christian Turner, Dick's chum from college days, is here, having driven down for the weekend. The Allens, the Braumillers, Bill Applewhite. Others. Gnats drive most of the guests indoors—but first, Dick says, everyone has to take a turn at viewing the sky through his telescope, now protected by a small cinder-block dome. Inside the house, even with the windows open, the cigarette smoke grows thick and ropy. Note: A cigarette stubbed out in the potted geranium. Someone sitting on the edge of the kitchen sink slipping backward into it, his legs dangling like faucets: hot and cold running. Drinks deserted in the living room because nobody can remember which is whose, until somebody comes along and polishes off whatever is left. It is July. Sonja creeps back out for some fresh air; she doesn't mind sharing it with the bugs. The moon has come up, round and yellow as a child's crayon drawing, a crayon moon, and it turns the neighborhood to cardboard, like a backdrop for a school play: white houses, black trees, shadows painted in the corners, flowers propped stiff and outsized against the dirt lane. The dirt lane looks as if it has been inked in with a Magic Marker.

"Where we are," says a voice behind her. Christian. She had not wanted to invite him, but he is in town and Dick was insistent. He puts a hand on her shoulder.

"Do you mind it? Being here," she says.

"No, I like it. Sonja—"

"Don't."

"Why don't you leave him?"

"Because. I don't want to, that's why."

He laughs. "At least you never lie, Mrs. Dawson."

She feels her face and arms relax. But she has lied, she is thinking. She lies to Dick and to Christian both by not asking about Miles.

"Unless you lie to yourself," Christian continues. "The real reason you don't leave him is simple inertia."

"*Real* reason? Inertia is a real and physical force."

"I know of stronger physical forces." He looks at her. "And so do you."

Does Miles still think of her?

She walks around to the dining-room window and peers in; it gives her a funny feeling, to be inspecting her own house on the sly, like a burglar. The rhododendron under the window is slick and cold to her touch, but her face feels hot: She can imagine how patchy red it is. She pushes the leaves away and takes a long look in. Dick is still wearing his chef's apron, and his shirt sleeves are rolled up above the elbows. He is talking with Bill—or rather, shouting at Bill. Whenever Dick tells stories, he shouts. Sonja feels her face flushing with embarrassment on his behalf.

She drops back from the window. "I'll race you," she says.

They have to be careful not to give themselves away, and run a silent race, legs pumping and chests heaving inaudibly, as in a dream-race. Sonja reaches the flower arbor first and crawls in. She is wearing a white skirt with little black Model T Fords printed on it, with a halter top. She takes the dress off and hangs it on a branch. She is in her slip. She takes off her shoes and lies down. Christian crashes in after her. Even in the dark she is aware of every detail of his presence: his supple back and narrow wrists, long legs and smallish feet, his green eyes, competent hands. He is defined by contrasts, a tricky kind of poetry. Right now, for example, having barely caught his breath, he begins plaiting three long fibrous stems he pulled from the floor of the arbor. When the weed necklace is done, he ties it around her neck, blowing lightly on the hairs at the nape of her neck. She reaches a hand behind her and touches his hand, and then she turns around to kiss him.

***

LINES. The old woman patting her coin purse like a pet: "There now, we'll be all right until the end of the month, won't we?" Watching the winter rain hurled down from the sky like iron spears.

***

That becoming human means learning how to die, over and over, on behalf of the one you love, and how to be born, over and over, on your own behalf.

***

FROM THE MARGIN. The active and passive linked through suffering, the act of undergoing and going under. What seems grim from one point of view becomes exhilarating when taken the other way around: the movement now toward creation.

***

CHARACTERS (cont'd). Sonja has the little Spooner girls over. She passes around a plate of cookies, while Dick pretends to be working at his desk. He pretends to be going over figures, but he is eavesdropping on their conversation. He would like to enter in but doesn't know how; little girls are peculiar creatures from another planet. He had been greatly relieved when his own child turned out to be a boy.

Trudy complains that her stomach hurts. Sonja asks him to walk both girls home. Pug gives him her hand to hold—it is so small, a miniature hand. He holds it carefully, as if it might break. He feels Sonja's eyes on his back. (Note: Another reason Dick stays with Sonja is that he loves her.)

Returning, Dick looks around him. The lawns are freshly mown, flowers fill the air with fragrance, the park hides the highway from view.

And already night has begun its journey from the outer edge, ready to descend on their little neighborhood like a plague of locusts.

***

A TALE FROM MY CHILDHOOD. One night a nervous wind kicked up the hickory leaves Chabasinski had raked; his park was rife with blue shadows. Squirrels scampered over the dropped pine needles, looking for acorns. I heard a noise and went to investigate.

I took my time, enjoying the walk through the park. The night was cold. The house on the highway at the corner of German School Road was dark except for a light on the back stoop. When I was little, I thought God lived there, that it was our father's mansion. It belonged to a middle-aged pair of brothers. I ought to know their last name, but I've forgotten it. They kept themselves apart from the rest of us; the park helped toward that end, separating us neatly.

The brothers had always been polite but mysterious. The elder was plump, like a pear, and had thin hair combed into points low on his forehead. In his brother, the same features were softened, so that from a distance he looked like a girl with prematurely gray bangs. Garth, who lived down the road from them, said the younger one also had breasts and alternated shirts and slacks with skirts and blouses. I thought Garth was being nasty until I learned that the younger brother made regular trips to Johns

Hopkins for hormone treatments. After that we called him
Tiresias, which is why I can't remember his real name.

The brothers ran a drive-in movie theater out on the
Petersburg Turnpike and their house was usually empty in
the evenings, but this night I knew someone was in there.
Something or someone had made that noise. Holding my
breath, I crouched behind a tree stump. Just then Tiresias
appeared on the back stoop, a large object in his arms.

He paused for a moment, looking around, swiveling
his head inch by inch like a periscope, as if to make sure
no one was watching and the coast was clear. My legs
began to tingle, going numb, but I didn't dare shift
position.

He was moving now, coming forward in a slow and
stately manner, like a priest or pagan bearing a sacrifice. (I
knew I was exaggerating, but the general consciousness
that night is when things conspire against one, together
with my situation—illicit and subordinate—frightened
me.) Then I saw the object in his hands, in those
hermaphroditic hands, was a dog. A dead dog.

I started to rise, to say something. To console. Instinct
held me down.

The elder brother spoke. Now I could see him, dimly,
in the center of the yard. He had been there all along.
"Here," he said. He glanced down, bending his head,
indicating the spot with a nod, and I noticed a pile of dirt
at his feet. There must have been a hole in the ground next
to it. A shallow pit.

Tiresias dropped the dog into the little pit, which must
have been scarcely more than a depression. It landed with
a thud.

I felt queasy and wanted to leave but couldn't abandon
the images going through my mind. I saw myself cradled

in Tiresias' arms, flung into a hole in the ground. I chewed grass, there was a taste of mud in my mouth.

The elder brother raked dirt over the lifeless mound.

"You should have dug deeper," Tiresias said; his voice carried clearly in the frigid air.

"It'll do."

"I didn't say it wouldn't."

"Okay, okay, let's not bicker."

"No," Tiresias agreed, "let's not."

They turned back to the house.

I was going to get up, when the elder brother said, "I almost forgot—"

He had forgotten the rake.

This time I waited until the door opened and closed and the stoop light went out, and both brothers and the sinister garden rake were all inside.

The next morning I warned Elizabeth Allen to keep Ludwig indoors; she called the police, and we learned from them that in the past three months four dogs had been reported missing from our area.

When the police investigated, they discovered four graves, plus the one I had watched the brothers digging. What ultimately became of the brothers, I don't know, but I've wondered if they could be living together somewhere, say on an island in the sapphire-blue Caribbean, free and unremarked, as man and wife.

***

DESCRIPTIVE PASSAGE (*early evening*). The rain freezes, forming a crust on the snow. Trees clatter in the wind like pinwheels. Lit from inside, frost gleams golden and silver on the windows. After supper on Sunday night, children sleep under warm blankets on clean white sheets. Outside, forgotten, a toy red wagon lies on its side near a flagstone walk, two rubber wheels suspended in midair.

***

A CADENZA. There is someone you love; in the hollow of a log, you find him, where honey is; his heart's mulch for red roses. You find him in the beat of a bird's wing, in music, in mathematics, in shifting patterns. Shade on rock, wind over water, water over rock, fire, cloud, fog over dark pavement, drifting. Was Christ translated out of the tomb instantaneously with the prophecy's fulfillment? More likely, he drifted, the scattered, saintly molecules regrouping on the other side leisurely, knowing there was all the time in the world.

For time is God's. He has bought it back from the High Priest of Death. This is what redemption means; originally, the word referred to the ritual practice of exchanging silver for the first-born son, obtaining his release from the religious servitude he would otherwise be bound to. The son is time, all-time.

You seek him in a hollow log, in the house of the dead dog.

Writing is a way of redeeming time. You buy back time with words. Alas, however precious, their value is nothing next to the value of the one Word. What that cost God! His very existence. "The Word," John reminds us, "was God."

But what this means—what this ontophilology means—is that there is no conclusion, only resurrection eternal and a forever-beginning. The creation continues indefinitely, word without end, God speaking his own name, *I am*, because that is the point of it, text and texture. Like the voice in the bush, it is itself. God tells the one story forever, redeeming lived time. To what end? To no end.

Conceive categorically of a *not*, a denial, a full stop at the end of a sentence. "The rest is silence." The rest *is* silence—but not the movement, and nothing is, that is not in motion. You go in search of the ground of your being, and the way leads under a hill. Here then is the traveler's dream, here now, of the Word made flesh. This dream shapes you (you are the dreamer dreamed); it creates you, forms and informs. It's as simple as this. You love someone, and he is not you, and you are raised by the power of his imagination. Short of the nth degree, a white stucco house sits back from the road—German School Road. Sometimes Chabasinski lives there; sometimes you do. You step outside. February, and snow on the ground, blue as smoke at night. Next door, Joseph Allen plays the violin; he plays the Bach Chaconne. The notes follow you on your walk, perch in the pine trees like sparrows. You are wearing a quilted parka. You lean against a tree and look up at the sky. Somewhere overhead, Pioneer 10 plunges past Jupiter, bearing its forlorn message into the future.

PAPER ROSE

The stucco house, shrouded in snow, was set slightly back from the road. A brick walk led up to it. In the summer, clover grew in the spaces between bricks, and, if left unmown, spread out into shaggy patches over the yard and along the ditch.

***

Boleslaw Chabasinski's father was a grade nine at the Bellwood Defense Supply Center. Twenty-five years ago, in Poland, he had been a handsome, lazy young man with black hair and white teeth. He inherited a large estate and a minor title, both of which he forfeited when he brought his wife and her spinster sister to this country at the beginning of the Second World War. Mr. Chabasinski's job was to buy aerial film, oil drums, textbooks, screws, paint, and mess kits from manufacturers with the lowest bids, and then to ship them overseas or to military warehouses. Most of what he bought went to Vietnam.

Dave Yancey worked at the desk in front of him. Yancey was twenty-six; he shared an apartment with a boy who studied church organ. He was always late for work. He brought in photographs of his potted plants and his parakeet to show to Mr. Chabasinski.

Chabasinski nodded politely.

Chabasinski's secretary, Mrs. Landrum, wore elegant wool or linen suits, spike heels, and a black hairpiece that sat high on her own thick hair. She was thirty-five and plump, but her legs were good.

***

When Boleslaw Chabasinski was five, he went to Patrick Henry Elementary School, started piano lessons, learned to handle a jackknife, and fell in love with Emma-Louise, a girl three years older than himself; Emma-Louise went to Hollywood to become a movie star, and he never heard from her again. He read the adventures of the Hardy Boys and *Scaramouche*, dated a girl who used plum lipstick and swore, and when he was sixteen, he entered the University of Virginia.

***

The aunt still lived with them. Boleslaw's mother had, year by year, relinquished her position to her sister, until now she only knitted, or lay on her back on the bed, a cold compress over her continually aching forehead, and listened to the light classical station supported by the Richmond medical profession. The aunt had bony red fingers. She clutched her shawl, which she draped around her shoulders even in hot weather, and cleaned house and fixed the meals. She changed her sister's compress, saying "Poor soul," and "Poor dear."

She felt there was a story in her life. When she was sixteen, she had promised herself to the son of friends of her father. The boy lived in Kraków. He was brilliant and sickly. He had impenetrable, marblelike eyes that made him look like her idea of an alien from another, a cloud-covered, planet. He died when she was seventeen. No one had known of her promise, it was secret between the two of them, but she never allowed any man to touch her.

When there was snow, the aunt sat by the front window, clutching her shawl with her bony fingers and looking out.

***

The house was at 610 German School Road. Mr. Chabasinski had remodeled the attic and built bookshelves. Without Bo, who was in Charlottesville, the three of them slipped into the habit of skipping supper. They spent an hour together every evening in the living room. The snow devoured the lawn.

***

"Memo, Mr. Chabasinski." She wore a green suit and her black hair seemed to burn, the way it shone.

"Fruit flies?" he asked.

"Again," she said. "You guessed it."

"I guessed it," he said. He carried his lunch to the cafeteria. He despised the noise; everyone had to eat there for a week after each fruit fly memo.

"Nobody wants this war," said Yancey.

Chabasinski smiled.

"Isn't that right? Mr. Chabasinski? Nobody wants it."

"I have had a letter from my son last night," he said.

Mrs. Landrum was eating her lunch with three other women, two tables over. Dave Yancey went back to the line for a second milk.

It was a job that got on your nerves. It was better not to trust these—"dumb clucks," they were. All the same, you had to be careful to do your job right. He was only a naturalized citizen. The colonels and majors and captains had ruined Jackson, another grade nine, for, however absent-mindedly, writing an address on a bid. Altering a bid. If they wanted you out, you were out. Yancey returned with the milk. "He's doing good," Chabasinski said. "Well."

"But how is he?" said Yancey.

"He is well," said Mr. Chabasinski.

"Martin likes Richmond Professional Institute. Bo could have stayed at home and gone there."

"Martin?"

"My roommate."

"Oh." He heard Mrs. Landrum laugh loudly and saw her get up, scraping her chair on the floor. She walked out of the cafeteria. "Boleslaw likes mathematics and physics. That is not a school for those subjects."

"Martin is studying music theory."

"It would be nice to have windows in here," Chabasinski said. "It would be nice to see the snow falling."

***

He rode home with Dave Yancey; the wheels dug into the sand spilled on the streets. The sky lifted, and he could see the sun going down. Its purple rays splattered shadows on the pine trees that clumped in a small forest on the opposite side of German School Road.

***

The aunt said, "She's so tired."

He said, "Does she feel all right?"

The aunt said, "She's all right, but she's very tired. Her head is hurting her."

"I'll go up," he said. But first he smoked a cigarette.

He went to the remodeled bedroom, where she lay on top of the bedspread with a quilt thrown over her. "It's only a headache," she said to him. "I am so embarrassed. I don't mean I should always worry you."

He sat on the edge of the bed and held her hand.

"Did you have a good day?" she asked.

"Fair." He yawned. "It's always fair."

"Don't worry about me."

"Of course I worry about you," he said.

"These headaches mean nothing."

"We had to eat in the cafeteria again today. Dave Yancey preened. His voice gets on my nerves. Otherwise, it wasn't a bad day."

***

Bo Chabasinski was a handsome young man with black hair and white teeth, but unlike his father at his age, he was not lazy. He went to philosophy and fencing classes. He planned to major in mathematics, and hoped, then, to go on to law school. In his second year he was elected class secretary and edited a surrealistic underground humor magazine. During Thanksgiving, he hitchhiked to Washington, D.C., and during spring vacation he went to Fort Lauderdale. A heavy storm splashed over the windshield; thunder barreled overhead, a thudding noise like heavy artillery; and when they drove into Florida, the sun shone thick and hot.

He handed his friend a beer. The billboards seemed to swat at him as they drove by.

They joined forces with four men from Cornell. They slept in one room in a motel, and Bo picked out a short girl with conical breasts. After each make-out session, she fondled them gently and ladled them into her bikini top. She pleaded with him. She said she was a virgin; he shrugged, and let her get lost again in the shuffle. He wandered up the shore. The faint plinking of guitars and banjos followed him, and he felt that there was no place for him on earth.

***

Mrs. Landrum sneezed; a few strands of black hair fell loose at the nape of her neck. Chabasinski said to her, "God bless you." She smiled at him.

He turned back to the papers on his desk, but in his mind he saw Mrs. Landrum as a tree, round and slippery, leafy and full. He imagined that she might take root, that her toes might shoot branches through the white high-heeled shoes.

Yancey said, "It's true. All the Bellwood lines are going to be monitored. Sometimes I think we work in Siberia."

***

Mr. Chabasinski wrote to his son in Charlottesville: "Your mother is not better. Though I have begged her to see a doctor, she says still it is nothing. We have had a lot of rain.

"Now I am buying headlights. For what, I don't know. They (my co-workers) are some dumb clucks. We spend money needlessly; I think this war is being planned to last eight or ten years. In any case, I feel they would just as soon be rid of me. I am not being hypersensitive, but Beatty jumps on me lately. But do not let this bother you.

"In the evenings, I am reading *Anna Karenina* and *The Kreutzer Sonata*. You may not realize it, but Tolstoyism once was very popular. It seems strange now. When I was your age, even the Bolsheviks couldn't stop us from forming these small societies.

"We are all pretty well, thank God."

***

The aunt bent over to pluck a stray honeysuckle vine. She had to clip the tough cord with scissors. Gnats lit on her arms; the smell of honeysuckle and dust oppressed her. She went into the kitchen, poured herself a glass of pink lemonade, and carried it back out to the porch.

She compared herself with the sun: They both were life-giving.

She went to check on her sister, who, in the drapery-drawn living room, clicked her knitting needles softly. Occasionally the aunt would wish her sister were well, and smiling, and confiding. She herself was basically generous; she would like to talk with someone.

She strolled through the semiformal park that Chabasinski had made of the empty lot next door. He had bought it for very little because it would not percolate.

The sun at noon stood like a sentry over the brown grass and pine needles. It entered her soul, and she thought it was strange that at her fingertips she ceased to move in time and space.

***

Red and yellow leaves, pitched by the wind, slapped against the red brick building. Bo put away his fencing gear. Tad said, "Pooltime, man." "No." "Why not?" "I've got a paper." "*Come* on, man." "Tomorrow." "I can't believe you!" said Tad. But Bo was thinking of his father, of his father's most recent letter, and of how the gulf between them was widening, but widening under a still, white mist, a fog that seemed to eat up the horizon, until nothing was visible but slow waves.

The corner pool hall was full; they waited for a table. Bo was introduced to a blond girl from Hollins College.

He took her out for a sandwich and a draft. She said, "I'm planning to be a political cartoonist."

He saw the answer she expected. "That's very unusual," he said.

"I already have a job lined up."

"That's good."

She lit a cigarette. "I believe a person should be realistic." He whistled inwardly at her vulnerability, was stung with a desire to protect her, and fell in love with the tenderness she drew from him.

"Yes," he said. Her hair got in her way when she leaned over for the ashtray. He pushed the ashtray toward her. He noticed the powder clinging to her nose and chin; she nearly lacked eyebrows, and he decided that this gave her an aristocratic look. He raised her chin with his finger, and he said, "But I—*I* want to go to the moon."

***

Chabasinski felt all the time that someone was watching him. He noticed that when he was absent from work for a day, when he got back, the papers on his desk and the files in his drawers would not be exactly as he had left them. Al Buchanan was downgraded and a guy from Accounts Receivable was transferred to his desk.

In the evenings, Chabasinski watched the moon bob up and down among the watery clouds. He gave Mrs. Landrum an English translation of *The Kreutzer Sonata*.

***

The aunt wished she were in Poland, if only for one more winter. She would walk through the old quarter of Warsaw, what was left of it, and, walking by the fortress wall, she would remember him, and also her father, who had been a brilliant, forceful man, a strong man, whose opaque, gray eyes had seemed to her fixed on some inaccessible region knowledge of which was not allowed to her. She would drink hot tea at a crowded café. She would sit at one of the miniature circle tables with two young boys and their dates, and listen to them talk about philosophy and their parents.

***

"How do you like these?" said Yancey.

"What?"

"They're nice, I think. I took them with a Polaroid. I bought it Saturday."

"They're very nice."

"You look worried."

"The color is good."

"It's a good little camera, in my opinion."

"Where is Mrs. Landrum today?"

"I don't know."

"Is she ill?"

"I don't know."

"Excuse me. I am ringing Minneapolis."

"Beep, beep. You can tell when you're being tapped. You hear a beep, beep."

***

His wife said to him: "The trouble is, I love you and you do not love me."

"No, that isn't true."

"I think this is the thing that has been wrong all along. You can't help it; it's not your fault. No one can help it."

"Will you let me call a doctor?"

"I am only tired."

"You should let a doctor come. It could do no harm."

"No. But I would like for you to read to me."

***

Bo and the blond girl from Hollins sat on the black iron railing in front of the Diner. He said to her: "I like to read. I like Tolstoy, Hume, and Brecht."

She said, "I do not like Shaw."

They marveled that their tastes should be so similar, and they went to a movie.

Afterward, they went to his room for coffee; they shut the door to block out the out-of-tune guitar whose weary song wandered aimlessly down the hall. He said to her, "I am tired of folk songs. I am tired of the people who sing them. I know that I have some real work to do, something important, and though you may think I fit in with these people, or even that I am, you know, 'popular,' it is all a pretense, and my course is merely tangential to theirs."

***

Chabasinski read to his wife until she fell asleep. He pulled the blanket tightly around her and kissed her on the forehead. He lit a cigarette and let it burn down in the ashtray. From the dormer window, he could see the stars flashing, like explosions too far away for the sound to reach him; and he believed that they were bombing the heavens; and he felt that they were shattering his piece of mind.

***

The aunt said to Chabasinski: "Lately you have looked very worried about something."

"She is quite ill, I think."

"But that isn't all?"

"No."

"When we were in Poland, do you remember! I wish we could go back. It could be I am getting old! They say one's childhood is closer to the heart when one grows old.

"My hair was naturally curly. It took fully half an hour every morning for me to put it up. How young I was!"

***

He watched her as she reached down to the bottom left-hand drawer of her desk. Her green wool skirt strained against her large thighs; he imagined he was rubbing that warm flesh and his hand sank into it like a ship into the sea, and the waves closed over and he was drowning.

She smiled at him. "It's back to the cafeteria, Mr. Chabasinski."

He nodded. The words rolled around in his head. Back to the cafeteria. Cafeteria. Back to the cafeteria, Mr. Chabasinski. He thought: Is my name Chabasinski? How strange.

He thought: If I were a poet, I would strangle time.

What does the poet do? He takes time by the throat; no, he puts it to sleep—in a Procrustean bed, and he chops off the head, or the feet or the ears, and fits it to the frame. I will sing a swan song for Time.

He thought: I have lost my sense of touch, of taste, of smell. I do not hear or see. The time and space I move in are surrounded by an old fortress wall that seals me off from the rest of the world.

The late-afternoon dust settled on and over his desk and dimmed his eyes.

He said to himself that his wife was getting better.

***

The aunt to her sister: "Today you look better. There is pink in your cheeks."

"Do you hear? It's Chopin."

"It's very pretty."

"When I listen to it, I think that we are all in a dream that God is dreaming. You and he and Boleslaw. Read Boleslaw's letter to me again."

***

Chabasinski called the doctor. "She'll be angry with me," he told the doctor when he showed up on the front stoop with his black bag, "but she is getting worse, not better."

"She needs to be in the hospital," the doctor said. "I need to run tests." He stamped his feet on the rubber mat.

"She will not agree to that. I think she wants to die."

"But she has you, her son."

Chabasinski hung up the doctor's coat. "We are not such prizes," he said, sadly.

He waited outside the bedroom while the doctor examined his wife. Afterward, downstairs, the doctor said again, "She has to have tests, X rays."

"Can you give her medicine for the pain?"

The doctor handed him two prescriptions already written up. "Bring her in as soon as you can."

"She won't come," Chabasinski said. "She says nothing's wrong."

"Do you think nothing is wrong?"

"I think she is dying."

"She is dying," the doctor said. "Bring her in."

***

She refused to go. She didn't want tests or X rays. In Polish she said, "Grant me some peace, my darling, that is all I ask. I don't want to fight. There was enough fighting, enough running. I don't want. No more, please."

***

Snow covered everything in sight: the forest across the street, the house, the semiformal park. The sounds of jet planes and dogs were smothered in the snow.

Chabasinski had told the aunt that her sister was dying, but she would have known it anyway. She knew, too, that Chabasinski was each day less within the world. His gray eyes seemed to turn inward, and she saw that he walked slowly from room to room, like a blind man, unsure of his way.

She felt that she was expected to do everything alone, and that this burden was at once unfair and unavoidable, that it was intolerable.

***

When March came, the snow melted. The water sank into the ground, and crocuses and jonquils bloomed. The sun drew the water up; there was a warm wind followed by rain.

**

Bo and the blond girl sat across from each other in the library. The rain slapped against the side of the building. The librarian went from room to room flicking on the lights.

He scraped his pen across the yellow legal tablet in front of him, but he hardly realized what he was writing. He felt happy and serious at the same time. He felt he could do anything in the world, if it were worth doing. For the time being, it was enough to be alive and see the gray sky outside and the bright lights inside.

**

Chabasinski dreamed that huge, fleshy birds flew over him, their shadows plunged him into darkness. He cut his way through the bushes, but thorns and briars dug into his hands, and the sweetness of strange flowers overpowered him.

The wind whirling into his room sent old bills and letters spinning over his face. He woke.

He wrote to his son: "Do you find that you and I are no more so close as once we were? But this is as things have always been. The father dies while the son grows.

"Perhaps I am a sentimental fool.

"It is hard to say. What do I know? I know that when you were little, we used ration coupons to buy milk and butter.

"Well, you will have to come home soon. Your mother will not last for many months more. I have sometimes thought that she refuses to live.

"She never wished we should come to this country. Like a flower, she could not stand to be plucked from the soil she was raised in.

"Well, it is late, they are asleep, and I am talking to myself."

***

The new buyer haunted Chabasinski; he knew that his time was up; he knew that he was the real outcast.

Mrs. Landrum hummed to herself and Dave Yancey asked her to be quiet.

Chabasinski imagined that her green linen suit fell from her in small strips, and she swelled up before him, the sun melting her pink skin into a stream of hot, bubbling blood. He imagined that some night he would seek out her home, enter her room when she was by herself, and while she clutched her throat, unable to move or make any sound, he would wrap his hands around her breasts. Her rapid breathing would pass into his mouth, and he would laugh.

***

Bo listened to her questions, but he heard only the sound of her words, like the faint background humming of crickets and mosquitoes on a spring night.

"You know how it is," he said. "I don't belong at home anymore."

She pressed closer to him, and he decided that he really was alone in the world. He felt sorry for himself. She kissed his toes and then his ears and his eyelids; her soft giggle grew thicker than he had dreamed it could, and he wrapped his hands around her yellow hair. He was in love. Never in history had anyone known what it was like to be both slave and subjugator of the same small, priceless, remote realm, but he'd write books about it someday, when the weather was right and his head stopped spinning.

***

Chabasinski sat on the lid of the toilet, staring at the bare bulb shining over the medicine cabinet. Green, black dots, butterflies would flit past his eyes. He shut them out. He tried to tie up his thoughts into some sort of bundle, any sort of bundle, but his head was spinning, and there was no one thing he could latch on to, until Mrs. Landrum, like a vast pink continent veined with blue tributaries, loomed before him, close at hand, and he felt himself slipping overboard, stroking his way upward to that thick, beating, fine heart. Then he thought: I am a silly, aging, dumb cluck; I am no good. But it was too late to stop.

***

He had let his life slip out of his hands. He had handed it over to history. The government there, the government here. Others were always in control. Somewhere along the line he had stopped trying to change anything. He had been derelict as a husband, negligent as a father. He had drifted.

***

The next day, Chabasinski sat in the cafeteria with Dave Yancey. Yancey's chatter slid along the edges of Chabasinski's consciousness. "It's stupid, yes, in fact, stupid. There wouldn't ever be any wars if it weren't that some people make money from them."

Mrs. Landrum waved her hands in telling an anecdote to her girlfriends. Chabasinski caught her eye and smiled politely. He said to Yancey, "It would be nice to have windows in here. Oh. It would be nice to see the sun shining."

He waited until he'd heard the first beep on his call to Minneapolis, and hinted that he was open to private persuasion. His salary was too small. You knew how it was: an ill wife, a son in college, the old aunt. He could arrange something, after all, they would find it satisfactory. Yes, he had the bottom-line figures on the bids. Would so-and-so have dinner with him? He gave out his home address and telephone number.

Riding home with Yancey, listening to the tires run through fresh, drying puddles, he felt sleepy and peaceful.

***

In the evening, the aunt called the doctor, and the doctor said Mariana would leave soon. Did she want her priest? Mariana said: "No, I am too tired; besides, what is heaven to me?" She asked to see Boleslaw. The aunt kept trying to telephone him, but there was no answer, only the forlorn ring, a futile, parroted question. She sent a wire. Later she talked with Tad, who said he would go to look for him.

Chabasinski said to his wife: "Here. I'll read his last letter again."

***

The aunt scuttled around the house, clutching her black shawl, until she had completed the funeral arrangements. Then she had nothing more to do. She sat in the Boston rocker by the living-room window and let the quiet spring breeze creep over her face. Her fingers grew numb and her legs grew rigid. She had nothing more to do. The light in her gray eyes faded as they fastened onto a vision; she saw her father strolling by the old wall in summer, and the young boy said, "Well! You were long enough, weren't you?"

***

Bo and the blond girl from Hollins College walked hand in hand down the dark, abandoned street.

"I'll tell you about mathematics," he said.

She glanced at him sideways.

"Supernovae are the thing."

"Why?" she asked. "I think you're mad."

" 'Mad…? Mad indeed. But observe, how they do light up the sky.' "

"You could buy me a present. Something inconsequential, just something little; you know, something from you to me. I would like a paper rose."

"I'll buy you that," he said. "I'll buy you a paper rose." He looked at her clean hair gleaming in the still night.

"What are these things?"

"Supernovae?"

"Yes."

"They are stars that overshoot themselves; they explode with immense force, and then they die. They aren't common. Other stars explode and die, too, but not so brilliantly."

"Are they rare?"

"As rare as kryptonite. As rare as you."

"How sad. But then it is not such a rare thing."

Her gold hair brushed his arm. Across the street, three soldiers waved to them, and they waved back, and as the soldiers moved on, Bo felt closer to her.

"When such stars die, their essences, their personalities, may hang on, may continue to assert themselves, as gas clouds, glowing, elegiac, aloof. Tycho Brahe wrote *De Nova Stella*—I don't remember when; sometime after 1570."

"*De Nova Stella*. It's a pretty phrase."

"But supernovae are not new; they are old and dying."

"Maybe you should give me a paper star. The Japanese make them."

"Tycho fought a duel over some mathematical point. He was nineteen, and he lost his nose. So then he had a nose made of gold and silver, and he wore that."

"You are mad."

He smiled. "It wasn't me. I'm just reporting the facts."

She had stopped in front of Mincer's Pipe Shop to turn toward him. Behind her back in the display window were issues of *Playboy*, poetry paperbacks, Grumpy dolls, hookahs, and folk albums. The night held a soft, damp smell, but the sky was clear. He scooped up the hair that rested in front of her shoulder and he pretended to study it. He thought he might cry.

"I'd like to marry you, if you would have me," he said.

***

Tad told him he had to call home.

Bo said to his father: "I'll be there on the next bus."

His father said, "Yes, you must come back now. I have something else to tell you."

Boleslaw didn't ask what. His father waited, and then said, "I am being fired. Oh, I am sure of it. I knew that it was my turn."

Chabasinski said: "Anyway I have framed myself. Do you believe in atonement? Never mind; you will.

"Yes, I am fine. Chabasinski is fine. But you will not be able to return to the university. I am sorry. I could not make everything right, only a little part of it."

***

An hour before the bus was due, Boleslaw locked his door, and with his secondhand duffel bag slung over one shoulder, walked back out into the night, only it was now early morning. The black sky was lifting in patches, but the stars were still out. He had made a paper rose for her and left it on his pillow, next to hers, while she slept.

He stood on the sidewalk. A car drove by. He shivered, and he could swear there was a cold east wind crawling around his legs.

LANDING MILES

Goldie Bangs's first love was books. One of the fringe benefits of marriage to Miles was that she got to stay on at the college after she was no longer a student. Every day she went to the campus coffee shop for lunch. Rainy days were mostly spent in the reading room of the library. Other days, she would go for walks in the woods that camouflaged the tennis courts. The campus was shaggy, ragged. Roses climbed the porchwalk between senior dorms, and halfway down the hill there was a remodeled carriage house for the luckiest students. She had been one, and a senior honors student. She'd shared a room on the top floor with Betty Lou Baranov. In those days they played *The Four Seasons* day in and day out, and she still heard the massed strings in certain weather, or, hearing them on the radio, instantly remembered how the dewy roses smelled in the early hours of a long day unbroken by classes. And in the redolent air of late summer and early autumn her stride lengthened and she felt energetic and anticipative, as if nothing was impossible. She still felt that way more often than she could tell Miles. He knew her instinct for freedom and was afraid she would act on it— he had told her so. What she couldn't get across to him was that the freedom she sought wasn't social; it had to do with the sense she had, at certain entirely unexpected moments, that she was on the verge of breaking out of her own body, so that if she could only find within herself that minute but absolutely crucial missing force and bring it to bear, she might escape herself once and for all and experience life directly, free of the distortion that went hand in glove with sensory mediation. She considered her body a clumsy thing, a nuisance at best and on occasion the worst dampener of her spirit there was, since it impaled her upon fallibility as finally as the butterflies in her collection were pinned in their cases. If Miles said she was as pretty as the North Star on a clear, frosty night, she was grateful for the truth of his statement but knew it to be beside the point. His love for her made her impatient.

It was five o'clock, the hour when shadows take on new shapes, become deeper, wider, more profound. The birdbath in the backyard had been vacated. Silence hung from the sky like sheets from a clothesline on a still day. Goldie gnawed the skin at the side of her thumbnail. Miles was in Newport News, attending a symposium on marine biology, and wouldn't be back until morning. She fed the hamster and the budgie, went outside to switch on the sprinkler system, and returned to the article she was reading. It was on the phenomenon of phosphorescence, and put her in mind of the first term paper she'd ever done for Miles. She had been trying to get his attention, but without success. Even though it was supposed to be a major *faux pas* to call a man, she had considered doing it, but she thought she might scare him off. But she could do something outlandish with the term paper and he would have to sit up and take notice. Using the red half of her ribbon, she'd typed the title on a page by itself: "Are Fish Human?" Ten pages later she reached a conclusion. "On the best available evidence, then, it seems safe to say that, all things considered—all relevant things, anyhow—fish are not human, and are not likely to become human in the near future, though they may have done so in the past." He refused to give her a grade on something so off-the-wall but asked her out. He was handsome, shy, a master of flourish, the confirmed bachelor surprised by circumstance. She was the circumstance. Betty Lou said rumor had it that Dr. Bangs carried a torch for a

Norwegian. That had made Goldie suspicious of her own good looks: Her hair was so bright it blurred into silver, like the sun at noon. Except on the hottest days she dressed in blue jeans and a red plaid Pendleton shirt. The sleeves were too long and had to be rolled up; but then, in other weather, she could pull the cuffs down over her chilled fingers. She spent a lot of time outdoors—the outdoor world was a gift from her father, a rancher in Arizona, and one of the things she and Miles had been quick to share with each other. She loved the outdoors almost as much as she loved books. It was as if Miles had given her the same perfect present a second time, with all the delight from the first intact, but this time the present came wrapped in Linnaean nomenclature, similarity and difference categorized and clearer than ever. "Look at this," Miles said; "see here and here." And everywhere she looked, the clouds opened or the trees bent back or the waves parted to let her pass. She decided she was chosen. Surely anyone would have, in her shoes. Chosen for *what* was an altogether different problem. Insofar as purpose was allied to function, it was in fact the problem of classification.

There were short-sighted skeptics who thought that classification was a supererogatory exercise, unnecessary and misleading. A rose by any other name would smell as sweet, wouldn't it? But perfume was not the point but only a secondary characteristic. Goldie knew that the point was in the naming, and that Adam and Eve, assigning birds and beasts to their proper phyla, had themselves co-created the universe, however fractional a part of it Fredericksburg might be. They were the first and quintessential scientists. Shamed by knowledge, they were raised up by the utter bravery with which they confronted more of the same, moving on into that tangle of theory and fact that stretched out from Eden like scrub country. Nobody knew what lay out there: flash floods, drought, and sudden drops off the scale of probability into the absurd. The rose was a rose until one day it wasn't, becoming instead a new and subtle variant with a treacherous tendency to cross the boundaries of established category. Viruses are living organisms, when they aren't inanimate objects, complex proteins. Light is a particle, when it isn't a wave. Like induction itself, science could be trusted only so far. Beyond that point, the gates closed on Paradise, and you were on your own in unsettled territory, and the sun might rise tomorrow, and then again it might not. Some days you couldn't even know for sure whether the sun shone or didn't. On a warm and windy day, when the light was as skittish as a colt, Goldie had gone to the class picnic with her handsome fiancé. So many changing shadows, ducking here and there, put her in a playful mood, and the quickening breeze lifted the hairs on her arms. She felt as buoyant as the milkweed blown on the current by the faculty kids. Her engagement ring winked and seemed alive, like a drop of pond water under a microscope, as she came up over the hill and joined Miles under the mulberry tree. He was talking to Christian Turner. "—Sonja," she heard Christian say. Goldie didn't like the man. His voice was too loud, and he had a habit of sucking his lower lip between his teeth, as if to suggest something. "What about Sonja?" she asked, coming up next to Miles's shoulder. "Sonja who?" "Oh," Miles said. When he waved his arm, as if to brush the question off, he hit her in the stomach. She laughed. There was a pause. "Sonja Henie," Christian said then. Christian's eyes caught the light from the southwest and turned as green as the glass of a broken Coke bottle.

"Forget it," Betty Lou advised her. Goldie agreed the past was irrelevant. "Besides," Betty Lou said, her chin squashed into a turkey wattle while she clenched the pillow with it and changed pillowcases, "if Dr. Turner said it was Monday, we'd know it was any day of the week but. He knows we know that. He's relying on it to upset you." Goldie nodded; the fact sufficed. She never argued with the way things were—only with the way they weren't. But persecution was not a member of the class of things amenable to analysis. It was simple, unpredictable, hard fact, the rough in the diamond, the thing you could never completely take into account in advance or dismiss afterward, the given, the doorway in the dark that transformed in a twinkling into a stranger with a knife. Evil was absurd; you couldn't dissect it like a frog, not even like the pregnant frog she'd carved open once, whose insides looked like a peanut butter-and-raisin sandwich. Its raisins had been tiny ones. She'd fallen into a reverie right in the laboratory, gazing so intently that the spots in the frog's belly became *muscae volitantes* and fogged her vision. Miles had whispered in her ear. He wasn't supposed to do that in class, but she liked him to. Nobody ever saw. The other girls had their heads down over their lab reports and failed to realize how serious things had gotten until Goldie told them she and Miles had set the date. It was the eighteenth of June. She wore laurel leaves and forget-me-nots in her hair, and a long white dress her sister had made for her. Miles was waiting at the altar. His curly hair had pins of light in it. She looked down the aisle, and the short aisle stretched into a vital journey; she was afraid she wouldn't be able to walk so far. Her father touched her on the back of her neck, as if she needed gentling, and he smiled at her and she at him. The pews on both sides surged with people. She was dizzy, the air was close, and one of the fans clacked along noisily at her back, like a lame horse. She was afraid something would happen to Miles before she could reach him, that he would vanish or be swept away in a pillar of cloud. But when she was halfway down the aisle he grinned, and she knew she was going to get there safely. She came up at his side, gasping a little, pitching slightly forward in step with her father, as if spurred on. The minister placed her hand in Miles's. It was well that he did that for her; she could not have done it herself, since her hand had gone as limp and clammy as a dead fish. Nevertheless, Miles seemed content to hold it, and when she looked at him, she understood how much he loved her and depended on her to be real.

HER, IN HIS STORY

"Eternity is passion."
—W. B. Yeats

She saw his films, read his books, was ravished by the way he could write about the suburban gardens humming in late afternoon, how when he walked out in them he realized the sound was lawn sprinklers. She carried on secret conversations with him, conversations replete with references to singing gardens and other things that were out of his work. Nobody knew this. Nobody knew what she was doing. She lived alone and there was no reason nor any need for anybody to know what went on in her mind. If she wanted to have an imaginary conversation while she washed the dishes or made the bed it was nobody's business but her own.

She imagined him in her bed. She knew she was older than he was, but perhaps not by too much. Anyway, for months, before she had ever read his stories or even knew about them, she had been half-wild with desire, for what she didn't know. For love, yes, but not just that. Whatever it was, it was something she must still be hoping could be found—she realized this, surprised—since, it seemed to her, we don't desire what we cannot imagine receiving. Wind blew in through the screens and hit her in the face.

She was a woman who had been hit by a man, but long ago. She was not a woman who had stayed around to let it happen again and again. There is a strength to be located in despair, and it gets you out the door. She knew perfectly well that when a man glared at you with contempt like that and with one vicious smack imprinted his palm on the side of your face there was nothing to do but leave. Leaving might be something you were ready to do or it might not; if it wasn't, you would spend months, maybe years, weeping over what had been lost, but you wept silently, secretly, and nobody knew it.

They might think they knew it but they didn't, not really.

They couldn't know it because they had not seen how his distaste for you yanked one side of his mouth down, a scowl/sneer/scornful scoffing. *That mouth you had kissed. That mouth that had kissed you.* It was a palsy of disparagement.

You left because when a man despises you all is lost.

Hate can be turned to love, but despisement and contempt cannot. Not any way she knew, at least.

A season of desire, she thought of it as: these months leading up to now, in which she had felt absence sleeping beside her at night, grief and longing walking beside her by day, the wind like a hand lifting her skirt. When she discovered his stories, she fled into them, away from absence, grief, longing, the wind and anything else that would assault, strangle, suffocate.

Although he had not imagined her, he had imagined a character imagining a hill like a teardrop, the long grass weeping, blue as water. Everything liquid and flowing and dripping. She imagined him imagining. She knew you could write shoreline hills and suburban gardens into the middle of a city. She imagined the stiffness in his shoulders from working all morning at his desk, the muscles tight in the back of his neck, the abstractedness he carried into bed at night. She was old enough to imagine other scenarios. He might be, instead of her lover, her son. She wasn't old enough for him to be her son, but she was old enough to imagine this alternative configuration of elements. Whereas, once upon a time, she would have seen him only in the one role: her lover, her hoped-for lover, a man with a talent for tenderness, capable of forgetting himself long enough to forget his fear.

Desire drove men into women but as soon as it was fulfilled they grew wary and wanted to leave. But she felt— she made believe—that he would want to stay and stay and stay. She remembered that moment when a man retreats from a woman's body as an abandonment, a rejection. She remembered it as a moment in which she felt stunned, as if hit, maybe murdered. Yes, it was as a dead person that she had sat up, the gism leaking from her and making the sheet clammy, and she felt as if she should apologize for that, as if it were her fault, this wanton exchange of bodily fluids, this overflow of passion, and she hooked her bare heels down on the inside of the bedframe and hugged herself, willing herself not to say anything, not to utter endearments or formulate claims or make demands. But also not to apologize.

In those days she smoked, and she lit a cigarette but her throat was dehydrated, and her mouth felt stretched and pulled, like some faded garment blocked to dry, from what he'd wanted done to him. Which was merely what they all wanted done to them—there were not *that* many scenarios. She could imagine being his sister, his daughter.

New York at night—in those days when she had smoked, she lived in New York—had been a place without parties, restaurants, theater, concerts. No salons, no gallery openings, no first-run films. It was simply a place where you worked a day job, a night job, a most-of-the-weekend job, trying to earn enough to get by on. The subway to work, to the second job, the bus home, buying Cheerios and cat food on upper Broadway at nine at night, the garish light in the store leaching the third dimension from everything, so that everything was depthless and transparent. Working at her typewriter on into the night, perhaps planting on the page, extravagant in the only way available to her, a garden in the grid of shadowy streets. She thought now of all the people she had never met there, because she had always been working except for the Saturday nights with men, all of whom were periodontally impaired or repressed or puddingy, or maybe only uninteresting-looking, and all of whom required perfection in a woman. The irony of it was, at the time she had overlooked their bad teeth or latent (as long as it remained latent) hostility or their love handles, or their being emotionally lethargic, but she could not overlook their requirement for perfection and her inability to meet it. She had smoked and hung her bare feet on the bed rail and her long, straight hair swept forward at the sides of her face, and sirens and horns had tuned up for the evening performance, an orchestra of traffic, but the man she'd just been with barely turned in his sleep, oblivious. Red lights on radio towers blinked against the black sky. She wondered where he was now, that man, although she wasn't even sure which man she was remembering. It had all been so long ago it was like a story, something she might read about someone else, another woman.

He wrote about women. He paid attention to their perfume, their hair and eyes, the different ways in which they asked for love. Some asked outright, laughing at themselves, maybe even at the men they slept with. Some blushed. Some hated their own neediness.

She never asked, she had given up asking. She pretended to a certain gruffness, making fun of anything she might feel. She was afraid her feelings might be a nuisance to others.

And yet she felt.

She felt, in his stories, a tremulous awareness of beauty that made her think he would know why he had written the particular stories he had written. When she set the soap back in its dish and peeled off the latex gloves she sat down on the kitchen floor, eye-level with the sink pipes, which were still sweating, and rested her forehead in her hands, thinking she could be in a story by him, if he knew her. But he didn't. He didn't know her, and therefore he did not know that she was, already, in his story and would be until the end.

After a while she got up from the floor and went upstairs to work, which she did in a small room the house's previous occupants had used as a nursery. When she was a little girl she had imagined that when she was grown up she would have twins. Twin girls. She was going to dress them in red and white polkadot raincoats. She had seen such a raincoat on another child and thought it was beautiful, the shine and slick and cheerfulness of it. It was *such* a beautiful raincoat she thought there should be two of them. Beauty was meant to be magnified, made more of. Her twins would be dark-haired. They would be talkative, at least with each other. They would have secrets but none from each other. They would have umbrellas. Rain would roll off the umbrellas and the twins would stay dry. When they got home from school she would see that they left their umbrellas open in the hallway and she would hang up their raincoats and serve them tomato juice, and crackers with peanut butter on them. When they took off the raincoats, the twins would smell, faintly and enjoyably, a little like rooms whose windows have been briefly shut against a summer storm.

She pulled the door shut and turned on the air conditioning unit. It was the only unit in the house, a small unit for this small room.

The room got colder. It got colder and colder. She put on a sweater. She wondered if he, too, could be in a small room somewhere with an air conditioner making it colder and colder. She thought not. She thought he was probably somewhere swank—a premiere, a book publication party. Or no—she decided he would be somewhere not swank at all. He would be visiting his parents, she was sure, in a rundown part of town, soot on the windowsills, furniture arranged to hide the spots in the carpet. The lace curtains snagged on a nail where a picture had been taken down and not replaced, the tea cozy in the shape of a camel. He'd be good to his parents, going to see them often, taking them out on the town now and then. They would look old but still be relatively young, perhaps not all that much older than she was.

An air conditioner was like a sea, drowning out other sounds. You couldn't hear a garden when the air conditioner was on. You heard the air conditioner humming, not the garden.

It was possible, she supposed, that she had gone a little bit crazy, but she knew that mostly she was just lonely. She didn't like to think about that now. What she felt now was simply this pain and longing, the pain of knowing life could have been different—was different for him, for everyone who knew him—and never would be any different for her, though it was probably going to get harder, because it got harder, and colder, for everyone, as time went on.

She tried to think of ways she might meet him. If she found out where he worked, where he lived. If she knew someone who knew someone who knew him, at least a little bit. If she did something that attracted his attention— but what would that be? What would cause him to turn his gaze from wherever he was in her direction and, seeing her in this faraway place, this place that was inland and like a coffin, notice that she was here?

She could think of nothing. She was completely dependent on him to notice her, to think of her, and he didn't even know this. He didn't know that she was out here, waiting in the margins of his life. She wanted him to read her. She wanted him to find in her a meaning like the meaning she had found in him. Then he would begin to love her the way she loved him.

Of course, she reminded herself, he might already be in love with someone. He probably was—men usually were. And having reminded herself of this, she put on a pair of gloves.

From the window of the small room, high above the street, she could see kids in shorts; drivers of convertibles with the top down and their left elbow where the window would be if the top were up and the windows rolled; small birds with dark crowns in a tree. The more she thought about it the more she realized he had to be in love already. His girlfriend or wife would be blond, or perhaps a redhead. She would be intelligent. She would be smart enough to understand him and keep him interested in her but not so smart that she distracted him from his own work. She would be kind, too, this girlfriend or wife, because if she weren't he would not have been attracted to her. In fact, it was her kindness that first attracted him to her.

So that was that. She herself was not, she knew, kind. She was mean, driven, and envious. She had tried to change these things about herself but failed, which left her feeling meaner, more driven, more envious. And perhaps she was not very smart, either. Perhaps she could think a thing through, all the way to the bottom, she gave herself that, but that was not the same as smart. To be smart you had to be willing to forget, for a little while, how other people felt. You couldn't be constantly worrying about them or gauging their reactions.

So maybe his wife or girlfriend was kind but not all the time, because sometimes she forgot about others; she tucked her blond or red hair behind her ear and smiled and said something bright and funny, and even if it wasn't kind it was so clever and entertaining that everyone forgave her, even the person she had hurt. When he and his wife or girlfriend got into their bed at the end of a long day—work, conferences, a meeting at the bank to refinance their mortgage, dinner with his agent—maybe even dancing at a private club later—he pulled her to him, fitting her small bright head into the place between his shoulder and neck, because a man in love needs to touch, a man in love doesn't want to let go.

A man in love had thoughts he wouldn't tell his buddies. Florid, floral thoughts. He thought about how embankments of flowers were like choirs, the deeper tones tall at the back, soprano peonies up front. He walked home instead of taking the subway or a bus or cab, because, even though he lived in a city where *urban renewal* was a synonym for *decaying infrastructure*, he thought the late-afternoon light edging the buildings was like a soft answer turning away wrath. A man in love was like that. A man in love noticed the white butterfly that strayed out into the streets, that it danced around the hood ornament of the passing car before it flew off again, weaving invisible currents of air into a single invisible braid. He noticed the way shoulders brushed his in passing, male and female shoulders, shoulders in sports jackets or Liz Claiborne dresses or bare beneath tank tops. He became conscious of his own body in a new way, and he fell a little in love with it, too, his own body, fondly grateful for the pleasure it could both provide and receive.

But a woman in love might never tell the man she loved. She might love in secret. She might love a man who didn't even know her.

And so he would go on walking home, and he wouldn't even know about her, anything about her. When he reached the entrance to the apartment building where he and his wife or girlfriend had taken a flat, he smiled at the doorman, and he stood to one side to let his neighbors in 5A onto the elevator first. When the lift's doors closed he felt suddenly fearful, as if something had seized him and was ferrying him to some unnamed destination, and his heart began to pound, as if on a door and demanding to be let out, but then the lift stopped at his floor and he got out and he walked down the hall and turned the key in his lock and went in.

She was already there, his wife or girlfriend, waiting for him. Even before she said hello, even before she moved over to him and lightly touched her lips to his, he admired the translucence of her skin, like a butterfly's wings, the answering softness of her hands. He was a man who had the good fortune to recognize and be pleased by his good fortune. He never wanted to run from the happiness in his life. Sometimes, though, he felt overcome by it. There were times when all he wanted was to cry, and he *would* cry, he would wait until he was alone and then step into a closet and feel buried among the hanging shirts and dresses and he would cry, tears splashing onto his hands as he covered his face. His hands on his face felt smooth, the palms like shell-less sea creatures attaching themselves to his clean-shaven cheeks, and deep inside the closet there was an odor like the sea in a cottage, the way the salt smell gets into the wood and revives whenever there's rain. It frightened him, sometimes, to realize how long and hard he could cry.

The gloves made it impossible for her to touch herself. And they were warm. But especially, they made it impossible for her to touch herself.

His wife or girlfriend—it was hard to see her, at first, beyond the bright hair, the smooth skin. Nice hands, probably—manicured, with the skin still fitting closely to the bone, even the knuckles. And her teeth would have benefitted from modern orthodontics, been straightened, whitened. No lines in the face yet, except for a few around the eyes when she smiled, and those were lovely, more like grace notes than like lines.

Her own face was vanishing. It was disappearing behind another face, one that belonged to an older woman. Sooner or later, the day would come when no one would stop to look at her face anymore, because it would no longer be there to be seen. And it had been rather beautiful.

His wife or girlfriend's face would fade too, but not for another twenty years. By then, she imagined, doctors would have devised or discovered a way to keep people from ever looking their age. Or if his wife or girlfriend did age, he wouldn't mind, because he loved this wife or girlfriend so much that he loved not only who she was but who she was becoming. If his wife or girlfriend cut or curled her hair it was a small change but one that added to his sense of her. Every change deepened her image for him, this portrait in time. He loved how she had been and how she would be, and this, to him, was what devotion was, staying with the same person as she changed.

He could tell that his wife or girlfriend had something on her mind, but he didn't want to press her. He wanted her not to feel that she had to tell him what it was until she was ready. He took off his jacket and threw it over the back of a chair and went into the kitchen. Little roach traps and ant traps were placed at intervals along the counters and floors. Pasta was packed in tightly sealed cylindrical containers with green lids. Light from a ceiling fixture streamed evenly down. All day, he thought, this room had been exactly like this, silent and still, though with the light off, which she had turned on.

In his work there was always the smell of water, a beach or strand, dune grass, often a ferris wheel or roadhouse dance hall. This was what he had known growing up—a sense of loneliness, people wanting a bit of fun, a band in the background, and later, after everyone had gone home, wind blowing lights in the dark water, a cruel moon, clouds shifting like moods.

But she was inland. She was so far inland that he would never find her, even though she was in his story. He didn't know, yet, how much had gotten into his story. He still thought that when he wrote something, that was it, but stories changed too, they began as narrative and then took on the multiple dimensions of poetry, becoming their own possibilities of being, ever new re-visionings of loss and gain. He thought he had written what he had written, but because what he had written had changed her, he had written her as well. The problem was that now she was lost. She didn't know what was expected of her, because he didn't yet know about her or that he expected anything of her.

On a hook on the back of the door was a coat. She put it on. There was also a wool scarf, and she put that on, too. In her scarf and coat and gloves she sat down at the computer, turned it on. It was still summertime outside. Her neighbors were still mowing their lawns. They were still having cookouts, grilling chicken with pesto. The twin

Korean toddlers rode their tricycles under their father's watchful eye. Now and then the father mopped his brow. This was not a scene that would be in a story by him. It was too inland, and too ordinary.

He was not an experimentalist. While he did intriguing things stylistically and structurally, style and structure were not the essence of his work, were not what made it extraordinary. What made it what it was, was its openness, a quality of attentiveness that amounted to receptivity. He was a person who could believe anything. He was willing to give up all his preconceptions and accept anything. This was how she knew he would accept her, *had* accepted her, even if he didn't know that he had. He had left room in his work even for her, the likes of her.

She had to be careful, she knew, not to upset the wife or girlfriend. She wouldn't want to take up too much space. After all, he had never *intended* for her to appear in his story, and he wouldn't want her to get in the way of the narrative. He had just left room for her, or someone like her. That's all.

So she wouldn't presume.

The thing was, to leave room like that was kindness itself, and no one should presume on kindness. No one should ever try to take advantage of someone's kindness.

She began to type on the keyboard. The gloves hampered her typing but didn't make it impossible. She felt the keys, through leather and cashmere, as padded, like cat's paws.

She was inland, even if the air conditioner sounded sealike.

She turned the unit up, as high as it would go. She was shivering, even in her coat and scarf, but her heart was on fire, it was a thing that had smouldered but not gone out and now flared up. There was a burning inside her that was a kind of localized hell, self-hatred an eternal penance, the flames of it eating at her forever. She had tried to be cold. Cold to herself.

Not to him, of course, but then that was an academic point, inasmuch as he was not someone she had met or ever would meet.

If she did—just for hypothesis' sake—what would she say to him?

Whatever her words might be, they could not be the words his wife or girlfriend said to him. He rested two fingers on that lovely left wrist when he came back out from the kitchen. She was sitting in the black leather chair. He had a glass of milk in his other hand. "What's on your mind?" he asked.

She put her gloved hands over her ears. She didn't want to know what was on his wife or girlfriend's mind. It would be something important, probably something that signified how much his wife or girlfriend cared for him. Or she was pregnant, and he would respond with delight and love. Or—but it didn't matter. Whatever it was, it would take him farther and farther away into that world where he lived, the world of premieres and publication parties, of women who were still young or youngish with bright hair and smooth skin and nice nails. It would take him farther into his own life, during which he would become famous—receiving awards and other honors—and then retreat a little, wanting to recover the excitement he'd had when he first began to write; and then, still later, when most of his work was done and his children were grown, he'd stand in front of the hall mirror, on his way out, and notice how his form had thickened, his jaw was a little jowly now, his eyes were tired-looking though he certainly didn't feel tired. He'd pick up his umbrella from the stand but wait just until he'd stepped outside to open it—some superstitions a person just couldn't shake—and as he walked swiftly to the tube stop, rain falling lightly with a hollow sound like flutes or fossilized bones, he remembered a story he meant to write, once, started, in fact, and then had set aside. It was around somewhere, in a drawer or filing cabinet. He thought he would dig it out and see if there wasn't something he could do with it. He thought he remembered that there had been something in the story worth working with, if he could figure out how to use it, though for the life of him he couldn't recall why he had ventured into that particular story in the first place.

He had never got used to the way ideas simply appeared. They were just there, like weather.

The underground stop was at the corner—a short walk, hardly long enough to follow his train of thought, beyond making a mental note to look up that beginning. *Lord!* he thought, dashing down the steps past a flower stall. *How beautiful to find flowers here, on the street, in the rain!* He had caught a glimpse of color—van Gogh yellow; pink so pale it was peach; and scarlet, crimson, and cerise. And the leaves! The leaves all washed a dark, deep green. It was a medley.

Then he was stepping onto the train, going wherever his life was taking him.

She waited to see where that would be. She had given herself over to his story and waited to see how it would turn out. (She wasn't worried. She trusted him.)

He was still seeing the colors of the banked flowers, their dampened leaves and petals, as the train entered the tunnel. If he wrote that story, he thought, he would put those flowers in it.

ART AND ABERRATION

*Divine Aberration: a small apparent
displacement in the position of a
heavenly body caused by the motion of
the earth and the finite velocity of light.*

It began with the letters. They turned up at the house, or at the school where we teach creative, as English departments are pleased to call it, writing. After a while it seemed as though the letters were following us. The letters were not, originally, something that happened in the normal course of a day. They became quotidian. We were put on our toes by the phenomenon, yes—we became alert, even apprehensive. We half expected to find these letters materializing out of the cold damp sleet-bearing air. We would plump up the pillow at night to find one underneath—the tooth fairy's literary cousin. We would discover the letters in our coat pockets. We would go to a restaurant and order steak and be served letters. None of those things happened, of course. The letters arrived only through conventional channels, each with the same return address in the upper left-hand corner, but it is important to understand the way in which they began to dominate each day as it was lived. The letters demanded attention. There was no possibility of ignoring them.

***

We live currently in the Fan District of Richmond, Virginia. It is an area of old townhouses, some renovated and some in pretty bad shape, that fans out: only two blocks wide where it begins, it spreads out to include more and more streets. Hence the name. Our house is three storeys high. It is made of brick. No two windows are shaped alike. We have owned it for two years now. Richmond is our hometown, and we are glad to be back after living elsewhere for some years. The pace of the place is right for us. When life moves too fast, there is no time to catch it on paper, and we are eager to catch life on paper.

Richmond has other attractions besides the livable rhythm. In spring, the city's median strips bloom pink and white and yellow, with azalea and mimosa. Hydrangea and lilac grow in people's front yards. In summer, the sun is gay. In winter, snow floats serenely down from the sky, lit by streetlamps, past the elegant and inelegant townhouses, and we are charmed. At Christmas time, there is a lighted candle in every window. It is the whim of the city council to advertise our city as the "city of candlelight." We do our share with candles in our own variegated windows. We would never let it be said that we are deficient in civic pride.

But—the letters.

***

They came well-spaced apart at first. Then they came at weekly intervals. Now they arrive daily. Each of them is masterfully cruel.

We were talking with a colleague about the letters. "Don't even think about them," he said. But that's easy for him to say. How could we *not* think about such blatant intrusions into our life? Letters, simply by virtue of being letters, require replies.

Yet to answer them would have been demeaning. It would have meant acknowledging the relevance of the criticisms if not their truth.

And yet, and yet—we were compromised in the mere opening of the letters.

***

Now, a scene, this scene: A woman is sitting at a table in front of a window, writing—a letter? a story? A story. Snow has piled against the windowpane in a pattern like tie-back curtains. Outside, the sun is shining ecstatically. Inside, the woman continues to write. A dog barking in the street punctures the silence in the room, as does the scratch of the woman's pen moving across rough yellow paper. On the right side of the table, next to her elbow, is a coffee cup; a spoon is making a brown stain on the table where it has been idly set aside. On the side of the table that is flush with the window, a jonquil sits in a jelly glass, stem snipped short for balance, the flower head bright and pert. But now the sun has moved so that it is in the woman's eyes, and she stretches out of her chair to pull the shade halfway down the window. Her attention is caught by the dusky quality this sudden rearrangement of sun vis-à-vis earth lends to the light that lies across the table like a tablecloth.

***

At first we had certainly *tried* to ignore the letters. But they refused to be ignored and in retaliation became more precise. They moved beyond the realm of professional concern to the personal. They tried to revise our understanding of ourselves in the pitiless light of their evaluation. We refused to be intimidated. We insisted on our right to interpret the past according to our sense of its movement into the future. Nevertheless, the letters continued to come.

***

The woman writing gets up from the table and moves across the kitchen to the gas stove. While she is boiling water, the telephone rings. She leaves the kitchen to answer it. When she returns, her face is changed: Delight has raised her spirit; she feels like Lazarus, newly returned, newly filled with oxygen, energy pumped into her lungs like air. She takes the pot of boiling water off the stove, fills her coffee cup, and sits down again at the table, using the same spoon to stir. Because of the phone call, she is seized with pleasure in the performance of all these small actions.

***

We composed an answer. *Dear Sir*, it began. *With regard to certain recent letters...*

***

The woman has her right eye squinched to the eye of a telescope in the dome in the backyard of a friend's house. The friend is male, married, about forty. His wife is in the house and knows that her husband is at this moment extending an arm around the younger woman's waist. The younger woman rejoices in the pressure of the man's arm; she finds it reassuring, stabilizing. The night is cold and both the man and the woman are wearing wool coats. The woman can feel the coldness of the concrete floor under her boots' soles. The wife is watching television in the living room. When the pair come back in, she will pretend nothing is wrong, nothing is amiss. They will both know that it is a pretense, and they will know that she knows they know. The wife is not amused by these moments of irony but neither is she overly concerned. She has long since given up caring. She tells herself.

***

The next letter made no mention of ours. It was, if anything, even more specific in its objections. We wondered if the police could arrest their author on general grounds of harassment, but we were too ashamed of the letters' charges to show them to anyone.

Each day became an ordeal.

***

Night was a sheet of carbon paper. Daylight—thin transparent onionskin.

***

The letters made no insinuations, innuendoes—that was not their style. They did not involve themselves with questions of relationship, affinity, love or hate. No, their objections were aimed at the target points of character, talent, and appearance.

***

At this point, into the story enters a new figure, a man of about thirty, a man with an acne-pitted face, a man with an automatic rifle.

***

The wife wakes out of a disturbing dream and rolls over to look at the clock on her side of the bed. 5:00 A.M. It is too early to get up, too late to go back to sleep. She gets up. She had been sleeping in her robe. It has become an old friend to her; she thinks of it as her security blanket. She slips into slippers, shuffles softly into the kitchen, and gets a beer from the refrigerator, opening and closing the refrigerator door as carefully as she can. Her husband will sleep for another hour, her son for two more hours. She pulls off the tab and drinks from the can. The sky through the window is barely beginning to lighten. The hum of the refrigerator is like a mantra. In her red robe and slippers, the wife is a focal point for the whole room. She begins to cry.

***

The man is lying in bed, awake, putting off getting up and facing his wife. He is sure she is crying. He knows she will have started on her first beer of the day. The bedroom faces the east and the blinds are drawn; he can see nothing in the room but everything in his mind's eye. He is thinking about the woman he is having an affair with. She would like for him to get a divorce, marry her. He is afraid of what this would do to his wife. He feels he must somehow be the cause of his wife's drinking and that he has a responsibility to take care of her. He wonders what a divorce would do to his son. Maybe nothing. Maybe his son would welcome the event. The house has not been a happy one for a long time.

The man knows he is not going to get a divorce.

***

As for the problem of the letters, when our reply had no effect, we wrote again, making a suggestion: We offered to meet with the letters' author.

***

The man is in bed again, but now it is not his wife's bed. It is 10:00 A.M. on a Monday morning. He does not have to be at work because he owns his own business. At the same time that his secretary is on coffee break, he is touching his mistress's hair, kissing her eyelids, drawing her closer. The sheets and pillowcases are navy with an Oriental floral design. He has told his mistress that the inside of a woman's thighs is the softest spot in the universe. Entering her is like going down to darkness and death. When he comes he feels resurrected.

***

After dinner that same night, the man steps out into his backyard to view the sky through his telescope. Cassiopeia is in her rocking chair; the Great Bear, hibernating, sparkles brightly. He enters the dome. This time his mistress is not with him. He adjusts the focus. The craters of the moon come into view, the lunar seas. The man's telescope gathers this far-flung light and transmits it to his eye. Before he goes in, he gives the telescope a loving pat. Both his wife and mistress refer to it in a patronizing way as his "hobby." He thinks of this small domed shell with its oblong slit for the long tongue of the telescope as a place of refuge. When he was a kid, he was enamored of Galileo and read everything he could find about him. His own son has no interest in astronomy. His son's thing is motorcycles.

***

The man with the automatic rifle is cleaning it, oiling and polishing it. He feels as if he is caressing it. He is doing this sitting on the side of the single bed in a room on the South Side.

***

The wife is watching reruns of "The Brady Bunch" on television. Her son is playing old Grateful Dead albums on the stereo in his room upstairs. She yells at him to turn the volume down, but he can't hear her over the noise. She swears and sits down again in front of the TV. She promises herself she will wash her hair tonight. Her hair is red; it has always been her best feature, but now she has to dye it because it has started coming in gray. Her red hair. The night she met her husband for the first time, seventeen years ago, she was wearing a black leather jacket, a black turtleneck sweater, a black skirt and boots. Her red hair, no gray in it then, glinting like copper, stoplight saying Go, spilled over her black-clad shoulders and black-clad back, and she knew red on black spelled temptation and danger. She had been wild and sweet, a belated beatnik, and now she is a middle-aged, middle-income suburban housewife and not-so-secret drinker. There are finely etched cross-hatchings on the pale skin of her face, and she wears glasses, medium-sized glasses with narrow translucent red plastic frames.

***

To continue. We received an answer to our answer. Really, it went beyond all tolerable bounds. There was a limit to what we could be expected to take.

The temperature had dropped, a nasty dive. The radiators in our house hissed. The house itself creaked from the cold. We made a fire, but even the fire seemed uncooperative, sullen. It kept dying out.

***

It is now Tuesday. The man is at his place of business, talking with his secretary. He is asking her to look up a certain file containing correspondence with a certain firm. When he retreats to his private office, he discovers that he is agitated, on edge. He cannot imagine why he should feel so jumpy. Then he realizes that his secretary is wearing the same perfume his mistress uses. This fact, that his mistress exists in a context of other women, that she buys and uses a product that thousands, perhaps millions of other women buy and use, profoundly upsets him. He feels he cannot afford to think about this.

***

The woman who was writing is now not writing but cleaning house. She derives a great deal of pride and emotional comfort from this house. Also, it is very near the place where her lover works.

***

The wife remembers the first house she and her husband lived in. They rented it from an elderly widow who had moved into an apartment complex. The wallpaper in the bathroom was hideous, with red, pink, and orange stripes, but they were afraid to hurt the widow's feelings by changing it.

When the baby came, they moved into a bigger house. This time they bought it. The wallpaper in the bathroom was fine, but they changed it anyway.

She had loved the new house before they moved into it. Then it had become something different, unfriendly—alive, an organism. It had fed on her. It grew warm and shiny and vital with her life-energy, and she had sensed herself growing colder, dull, angry. When she tried to explain this to her husband, he told her to get a job, get out of the house, do something. But what could she do? She had a baby. Now she has a teenaged son and her husband has a mistress. There is tit for tat somewhere in that. Tit for tat. She laughs.

***

The mistress would like to have a baby. Time is rapidly running out. She has tried to express her urgency to her lover, always keeping her tone light. Sometimes he goes away from her in his mind—she can tell. She can tell from his eyes, which are deep blue, from his face, which is worn, from his hands, where he displays his only sign of vanity in well-manicured, buffed nails. She is careful then to call him back with little jokes, asides, small indications of greater self-sufficiency. She knows he does not want her to be dependent on him, a drain. He already has a wife.

When she arrives at this last thought, she starts to cry, checks herself, and mops the kitchen floor. The sun is almost overhead, slanting through the window, its glare on the stainless-steel sink intense, demanding. Suddenly she feels weary and decides what the hell, the floor is all right without mopping.

***

We were describing the letters, how we decided to deal with them: head on. This time, therefore, we did not suggest. We simply announced that we could be found sitting in a certain restaurant at noon on a particular day. We picked a day some days away, in order to avoid conflicts with the letters' author's schedule, whatever that might be. We were unwilling to allow him to come to our house.

***

The New Year came and went. The candles were removed from their windows, the Christmas trees were stripped of their ornamentation and left on sidewalks for pickup, the downtown decorations disappeared. The city looked naked. No festivity about the town now! The starry nights no longer competed with the colored winking lights of Christmas, nor with candlelight. The earth had rolled farther along on its endless circuit, and the city was exposing its nether side, the grayish-whitish slush-brushed underlayer of the long turning year.

The sun came out, but still the snow refused to melt. Snow crystals scintillated among the massed dullness of snowbanks along the sides of streets. An exhibition of Chinese pottery opened at the Museum of Fine Arts. A new branch of the public library system opened on the expanding South Side; there was a brief ceremony and neighborhood reception; the mayor arrived late. Certainly nothing momentous in any of this.

A perfectly ordinary city, except in one particular: Unlike Moscow, London, New York, it happened to be where, at such-and-such a moment, *here* was.

It was now the twenty-third of January, a Wednesday.

***

The man who is loved by the woman who was writing is promising to drive his teenaged son to a motorcycle race track in Maryland next Sunday. The son is six-three, taller than his father, "and about three inches wide," his father likes to say. His father figures that being a participant in a supervised motorcycle competition is safer than being a sixteen-year-old automobile driver.

The boy is his father's most adored reason for living. Sometimes the father forgets this, but always the boy reminds him, merely by being, even by being a pain in the neck. Even the demands his son makes of him force him to recognize that it is exactly those demands that justify his own existence. He thinks there is precious little else that justifies it.

***

For the man who is a father is inclined to feel that he is a failure as a husband and a lover. He knows his wife and mistress cry when he is not around. He does not want either of them to cry.

***

Now:

***

The man with the automatic rifle has secreted the rifle under his overcoat. He has locked himself into a stall in the men's room in a downtown office building.

***

As in a rhyme, the woman who is married to the man who is the lover of the woman who was writing is sleeping next to her husband. She will wake early, restless, assaulted out of sleep by the twin desires that plague her, the desire to drink and the desire to stop drinking, a conflict that keeps her in perpetual turmoil, but for now she is sleeping, on her stomach, her right bare foot touching her husband's right leg, her left leg bent at the knee in childlike fashion.

***

The woman who was writing is also sleeping, in her double bed, alone. She envies wives, who sleep next to their husbands. She also luxuriates in the freedom she has, living alone, to be her worst self without reprimand. She thinks this must be the unhappiest restriction in marriage: being subject to someone else's approval or censure, having to look good, be good, do good all the time. She could never do this. She has said so to her lover, warning him against marrying her at the same time she pleads with him to marry her. He has told her that she doesn't understand marriage. She does not believe him.

***

The night watchman has made his rounds, and the man with the rifle is climbing the staircase of the office building.

At the top of the staircase, the man with the rifle breaks a padlock and steps out onto the roof. The night is extremely cold. He spends it huddled on the inside side of the door to the roof.

***

Everyone sleeps.

***

The sun comes out as if high-spiritedly in the morning. The temperature has soared to fifty degrees, a foresign of spring. By seven, the rest of the snow has melted away. The wife retreats to the bedroom, reclaims it for herself after her husband has left for work. Her son makes his own breakfast, grabs the lunch money his father has left on the kitchen counter, and leaves for school. His mother has not drunk her usual wake-up beer. She is pacing herself; she plans to do some shopping downtown today.

She makes up her face, pulls on skirt, sweater, stockings, shoes. Makes the bed. The silence in the house seems to emphasize the clatter in her own head—she feels as if she can almost hear her brain at work, thinking, gears grinding up for the day. She would as soon shut it down permanently.

The stores won't be open yet. She goes into the living room, sits down, picks up a book.

***

The husband is at work, finalizing the details of a contract with a subcontractor. He puts one party on hold while he talks with the other. The door to his office is partly open. He can see his secretary seated at her typewriter. She is wondering when would be the best time to tell him that he will have to hire a temporary replacement for her. She is pregnant and plans to stay out for at least a month after the baby comes.

***

The woman who was writing enjoys and prolongs the business of getting out of bed. She stretches her legs, turns on the bedside TV and listens to the news, and only then gets up. The bedcovers are rumpled. She stares at them for a moment, realizing she has never spent an entire night with her lover. Would she be less restless with him? More? She shrugs and gets dressed.

She pulls the kitchen window shade, lets it snap up. Sunshine plunges into the room, spilling over the linoleum floor like a wax.

She makes herself a piece of toast, eats a bowl of cereal, drinks orange juice, coffee. She is meeting her lover at noon. The morning seems long.

***

By eleven-thirty, the wife is on West Franklin. She discovers she has let herself drift into her husband's domain. She thinks briefly of finding a pay phone and calling him, suggesting they meet for lunch, then discards that idea as a bad one. He does not like to be called at work.

She has not actually bought anything yet; sometimes when she goes to town she comes home with nothing. But it is an achievement to have gone to town, to have spoken with salesgirls, moved among other lonely housewives, established for a while at least that the outside world is still there. She could use a drink.

***

The sniper is feeding the magazine into his M-16. He feels the sun's approach as he would any intruder's. He wishes he had brought shades, a cap with a visor. The sun ricochets off the rifle barrel, makes it look hot and sticky, the roof tarry.

***

The secretary is making her way into a crowded nearby restaurant, ordering a sandwich and soft drink to go. Waiting, she turns around and scans the restaurant. Her boss is here, in a booth on the side. She wonders if the woman he is with is his mistress—she knows he has one, has overheard whispered telephone conversations, sent flowers when he told her to. Taking a longer look, she approves of the woman's haircut, brown hair shaped in a pageboy, her face bare of make-up. She is too far away to see more than that. The woman in the booth looks up, catches the secretary's eye, her glance sliding away immediately, not recognizing that the woman at the takeout register is her lover's secretary. The cash register rings, bell-like. The secretary gathers her change, her order, and steps back out onto the sidewalk. It is now noon, and she walks slowly, liking the January sun's proleptic warmth.

***

It is a lovely day, the air full of the cool perfume of a spring day in the middle of winter. The secretary decides to eat her lunch in the courtyard that lies between the building she works in and the bank on the corner. She picks out a bench, takes her lunch out of the paper bag, unbuttons her coat but leaves it on. Above her, the sniper is trying out possible targets, fixing this person and then that one in the crosshairs. He has no intention of rushing, of hurrying over what he has for so long waited for.

***

The wife is trying on a dress in a boutique, one of the small stores on the fringe of the Fan District between the university and the downtown area. It is too young for her—too campy, too playful. The salesgirl asks if she wants it wrapped. She shakes her head no.

***

In the restaurant, we too were there. We had gone there to meet the author of the letters. We believed he would show up, if only out of curiosity, and he did.

We were calm, controlled. After all, we had had time too, time to decide what course we would follow, which responses we would allow him to notice and which we would keep to ourselves.

He did not look at all like the person we had expected. We had expected someone better dressed, with an air of authority, someone more commanding than that person facing us from the opposite side of the table. We were interested to know what this meant, this person's presence's being so plainly at odds with the voice in the letters.

There was an awkward lull at the start, and then we began to speak directly to the issue. We asked him what he wanted of us.

Greater significance! he said. More meaning!

We were ashamed, guilt-struck.

A deeper analysis of character, he continued.

We were full of remorse, and yet we asked how we could possibly have done any better than we had. We had done our best, we said.

Not good enough, he said, slapping his right hand down on the table top. He was holding a hot dog in his left hand.

He had gotten mustard on his tie—hardly the most dignified of figures. Yet he knew as well as we did that all power rested on his side of the table: We were the ones who had allowed ourselves to be scrutinized and judged. It had not been unavoidable. We chose to do what we did.

But it was precisely for that reason that we were so vulnerable. What we did mattered enough to us for us to have chosen to do it.

He was rubbing at the spot on his tie with a paper napkin he had wetted in his glass of water. While his head was down, we saw that he was going bald. This made us feel, however frivolously, surer of ourselves: He was as mortal and fallible and corruptible as the rest of us. We tried to hang onto this thought when he returned his attention to us.

Give up, he said. Quit. The world is already overrun with trivia.

We looked him in the eye. No, we said.

Well, that's a helluva note, he said.

Nevertheless.
All right, all right. It's your life.
Exactly, we said.
If you want to throw it away.

***

We said nothing.
I mean, he said, *I'm* not going to stop you. Jesus Christ, I've got better things to do with my time.

***

We doubt it, we said.
Aha. Sarcasm, the last line of defense for any writer.
We were realizing that what we had said could have been taken two ways, one against us. He was too stupid to catch the ambiguity.
Jonathan Swift? we argued. W. H. Auden?
Irrelevant. Objection overruled.
We decided to let him make the next move.

***

The sniper has placed his rifle aside again. He is experiencing the strangest sensation: He feels as if the sunlit air is water, and that he is floating dreamily upon it. He blinks his eyelids, trying to clear his head. His arms and hands seem limp, muscleless. Impotent.

***

The wife returns to the street. It is 12:55.

***

The wife's husband and his mistress rise out of the booth, put on their coats, and pay the check. While they are standing at the cashier counter, the mistress picks up two creamy mint patties at two cents each and glances at her lover, querying him with raised eyebrows. He smiles and tells the cashier to add four cents to the bill. His mistress gives him one of the mint patties and they both pop the patties into their mouths, slipping the balled-up tin-foil wrappings into their pockets. This simple action has much affected them both. They feel connected, alive, and for one memorable moment anyway, irresponsible.

***

It is 1:00 P.M. Only the son is not present at this next scene. It is he on whom the consequences of what happens now will devolve.

***

The sniper passes a hand over his eyes. He has resolved his intention, the purposive relation between himself and this place he is in. He picks up the gun, takes aim, flicks off the safety, and shoots.

***

The point is, the author of the letters was saying, some things are necessary, others are not.

***

We agreed. Our disagreement was only in deciding which was which.

An example, he said. Some writers of fiction are necessary, while others are not.

We disagreed.

Of course you would, he said. You would have to.

Not because of that.

What, then?

An example, we said, and we narrated a short story about a man, his wife, his mistress, his secretary, and his son. Then we got up to leave.

But the ending? he said.

Yes, we said. That's what you need us for. The ending.

A cheap trick, he said, scowling. A cheap trick. His complexion was bruise-colored, with a strong undertone of orange. He looked as if he was a candidate for a heart attack at some future date. He had those creases in his ear lobes that are said to indicate a weakness in that direction.

We don't care, we said.

***

The sun had moved behind a cloud, and it was winter again. Here we were, in the place we had started out from. We stood on the sidewalk, liking that melancholic mood. Then we went home.

***

Of course, we thought later, he made the mistake of taking us at our word. Maybe there was no ending, or none that we could tell. Maybe the ending was out of our hands as well. Who knew what ending a beginning might lead to? We were ourselves only part of a larger story, whose

ending we could not know, a denouement that would find
us whether or not we could find it. Such is the nature of
eschatology, or shall we say simply, the study of *last things*.
The conclusion, lost to us in mystery, reveals itself in the
act of self-knowledge, God's mind learning its own power.

Kelly Cherry has previously published nineteen books and eight chapbooks of fiction (long and short), poetry, essays, criticism, and memoir, as well as translations of two classical plays. Her most recent titles are *Girl in a Library: On Women Writers & The Writing Life* and *The Retreats of Thought: Poems*. She is Eudora Welty Professor Emerita of English and Evjue-Bascom Professor Emerita in the Humanities at the University of Wisconsin-Madison and now lives in Virginia. Her awards and honors include fellowships from the National Endowment for the Arts, the Rockefeller Foundation, the Institute for Advanced Study, the Dictionary of Literary Biography award for the best collection of short stories of 1999, publication in the prize anthologies *Best American Short Stories, The O. Henry Awards: Prize Stories, The Pushcart Prize,* and *New Stories from the South,* the Bradley Major Achievement [Lifetime] Award, a USIS Speaker Award to the Philippines, and the James G. Hanes Poetry Prize from the Fellowship of Southern Writers for a body of work in that form. She is currently a contributing editor to *The Hollins Critic* and a member of the Electorate of the Cathedral Church of St. John the Divine, New York.